STONE
M.I.A. HUNTER
ESCAPE
FROM NICARAGUA

JACK BUCHANAN

JOVE BOOKS, NEW YORK

STONE: M.I.A. HUNTER
ESCAPE FROM NICARAGUA

A Jove Book / published by arrangement with
the author

PRINTING HISTORY
Jove edition / December 1987

ISBN: 0-515-09334-3

Jove books are published by The Berkley Publishing Group,
200 Madison Avenue, New York, New York 10016.
The name "JOVE" and the "J" logo
are trademarks belonging to Jove Publications, Inc.

PRINTED IN THE UNITED STATES OF AMERICA

10 9 8 7 6 5 4 3 2 1

ESCAPE FROM NICARAGUA

Prologue

The Huey Cobra skimmed dark clouds, crackling with jagged streaks of lightning. There were five men on board; two were C.I.A. agents being sent into Nicaragua to contact a mountain band of Contras.

One of them, Don Shepard, said, "It's getting late. Will we make it before dark?"

"Trust me," the pilot answered. "I've been over this route a dozen times. I'll get you to the church on time."

The other agent, Jack Harris, said, "Aren't we pretty goddamn high?"

The pilot glanced at him. "Listen, you want to take over the controls? I'll curl up in the back there. I could use some sleep."

"Come on . . . I didn't mean nothing."

The pilot grunted. He was tired and wanted to set the bus down and have a drink. Instead, he was up in the fucking blue, heading into enemy territory to deliver some C.I.A. spooks to a postage-stamp drop in the hills. He didn't care for it. Especially when SAM's had been reported no longer than a week ago in the area.

He scanned the horizon and moved the controls gently to starboard, lining up two mountain peaks. His destination was just to the right of them. He glanced at his watch. They were probably twenty minutes to a landing.

In the control center on the rim of an active volcano, the Nicaraguan air-traffic controller fixed his gaze on the small blip as it moved down along the coast, flying just high enough to avoid the white-capped waves.

At the operator's left elbow stood General Romero Perez. He wiped his sweaty brow with his sleeve. The small room was hot, humid, claustrophobic.

"It is headed toward Managua," he said in his native Spanish. "She will fly along the coast, just outside our coastal limits, then cut in abruptly across the mountains to the capital. Let's scramble the Migs and shoot her down the moment she enters our air space."

On the other side of the radar operator Colonel Zharka, a Soviet "adviser" assigned to Perez' unit, shook his head.

"Nyet." He corrected himself and switched to Spanish. He tried to speak the native language wherever he served. "No. I want them alive. We shall put plan 'capture' into effect."

Perez showed puzzlement, then anger.

"I know of no such plan."

"The squadron knows. So does the commander of your helicopter gunships. Just call them."

"No. This is my country. I give the orders."

"It is your country only as long as we permit it to be so." Zharka reached for a telephone. He would give the order himself. But he tried to placate the general, too.

"The Migs will form a circle around the helicopter. Nothing can escape their encirclement. But their firepower is only for destruction. A helicopter gunship has many weapons. They can force down one of their own kind with less chance of killing the passengers."

He spoke Russian into the telephone.

"There," he said as he hung up. "It is done. In an hour we should have two live C.I.A. agents. Plus a pilot and copilot, hopefully alive. You will be honored in Managua."

"And you," Perez said bleakly, his eyes still on the radar blip, "will be honored in Moscow. . . ."

Aboard the helicopter the pilot checked his instruments. "Goddamn! They're locked on to us already."

His copilot leaned left and checked the radar detector. Its light blinked brightly. No question. A radar somewhere inland had picked them up as a telltale blip on its screen.

The younger man tried to hide the fear snaking up his back. It was his first flight into enemy territory, and he had been clammy wet in his own sweat since he had first seen the flight plan.

If the commander had given him more time, he might have feigned illness. He was sick all right, nauseated at the prospect of deep penetration into enemy territory.

Unbuckling his belt and unplugging his earphones, the crewman, a lean kid, left his seat and worked his way back to where the two men sat, both locked in their private thoughts.

Seeing them lifted the copilot's spirits. At least he wasn't them. He and the ship would be on the ground only long enough for the two men to toss out their ordinary-looking suitcases and jump to the ground.

They would be staying behind.

When they raised their eyes and escaped from their private thoughts, he plugged in his intercom cord and waited as the two men pressed hard on the side of their helmets. There was no other way to be heard above the roar of the engines.

"We've been picked up by enemy radar."

The two men exchanged glances.

"Have we aroused any suspicion or defensive action yet?" the older of the two men asked. He called himself Shepard this time, but he had been known by many names through the years. He was forty-five, practically over the hill in his business, and his face made him look older. There was a scar on one cheek and a general dry, hardness to his skin. Beneath his shirt and trousers were the scars of previous missions that went sour.

Impatiently he repeated his question. "Is there any sign that we have aroused suspicion or defensive action so far?"

Before the crewman could reply in the negative, the stronger, more confident voice of the pilot came over the intercom.

"I just got a report via satellite," he said. "Near as I can tell, three bogies just scrambled from the air base at Managua. They're no more than five minutes out. And I got something slower headed our way."

The crewman looked hopefully at the passengers.

Shepard said nothing.

His partner appeared disinterested.

"Well?" The lieutenant looked from one to the other.

"Well what?" Shepard asked.

"Do we turn back? In five minutes we can be back over international waters. They won't hit us there. Bad press. And there's two destroyers backing us up." He was talking fast, his frayed nerves showing in every muscle of his face. His eyes darted, his nostrils flared. "Don't you understand?" His voice became high-pitched and boyish. "They're going to shoot us out of the fucking sky!"

A high-pitched roar overpowered the sound of the chopper's engine. The craft dropped, throwing the lieutenant against the unpadded ceiling. He bounced back, slamming into the floor, then flew against the bulkhead and dropped unconscious. Shepard caught him and drew him into a plank seat where he could buckle him into a seat belt.

The crewman was out of it. He was barely breathing as a streak of flame cut across the starboard side, shaking the helicopter.

They'd been given the pep talk, the kamikaze lecture, the boys in the field called it. Die for the good U.S. of A. But don't get captured.

Shepard and Harris had nodded when given the order. They would have raised their right hands, placed their left on a Bible, and given their Scout's honor. But they weren't dying for anybody if they could help it.

And right now the question seemed moot as the night sky came apart with the thundering roar of jet engines, streaks of lightninglike flames of rockets and tracer ammunition. The American helicopter did a dance, slid off to the left, slid to a fast stop, and hovered briefly in the path of the oncoming jets.

"Yeah, they're bogies all right," the pilot said from the cockpit.

He remained calm. The whole sky was a mass of streaks and noise and confusion. If he expected to live for the next two minutes, he would have been a fool.

But then he had been at the embassy in Saigon when the helicopters snatched the last Americans and the highest-ranking South Vietnamese collaborators from the oncoming Communists. He hadn't expected to live through that either.

"Are they saying anything to you?" Harris asked.

He had taken off his seat belt and moved to the cannon position amidships. His partner took up a similar position on the starboard side. They would try to take one of the Migs with them if the whole mission fell apart.

"Yeah, they're talking to me," the pilot replied. "Spanish and Russian. I can't understand a fucking word."

"Give them the cassette," Shepard ordered.

In the front cabin the pilot ignored all the complex instrumentation and punched the play button of a twenty-five dollar tape cassette.

The message, garbled Russian, played into the radio transmitter.

"Mayday, Mayday," it cried in essence. "We cannot read you. Mayday. Ermine two heading for Managua airport. Clear the runways. Mayday."

For several moments the Migs continued crisscrossing the sky, but as they turned to take up perimeter positions like Indians riding bareback around the circled wagon trains, Don Shepard sensed disaster.

The pilot raised the chopper nose, braked his forward motion like a cat skidding on her claws at the sight of three Dobermans rushing at her across a barren field.

It happened too quickly to really see. The two Migs collided head-to-head. One minute there was a blur in front of the chopper. The next the sky exploded. Yellow flames. Popping fireworks. Then chunks of metal cutting, slamming, against the American chopper.

Big holes appeared in the windscreen.

The rest of the clear plastic spiderwebbed with cracks. Wind cut at the pilot's face, flooding his eyes with tears.

The last thing Shepard saw clearly was the moon-splashed waters of Lake Nicaragua, an expanse of water more than a hundred miles long and several dozen miles wide.

It was directly below him.

Disaster, he thought.

The flight plan had been simple. After signaling Mayday, he was supposed to send out the message that he'd be making an emergency landing, but he expected to make it to the international airport at Managua on the far side of the lake.

The lie would buy them time for their real orders.

They were supposed to go down on the sandy beach of the lake, then drop the two passengers and a barrel of oil to simulate a crash site. From there the chopper would skim the jungle growth and follow the lake south into Costa Rica.

The two passengers would have time to disappear into the jungle before the Communists reached the phony crash site. But the whole plan exploded on him.

They were already halfway across the lake.

And then, as he watched the burning jets plunge into the shallows of the giant lake, the pilot finally saw a slower craft off his right wing. A fearsome Russian Hind gunship had taken up an escort position off their right side.

Russian crackled in their earphones.

The other pilot wanted them down. Now. Not ten minutes from now. But now, exactly *now.*

A burst of cannon fire across the bow made the message perfectly clear.

From the rear agent Shepard said, as calmly as he could, "I got the Russki in the sights, I think." He wasn't trained in the use of the weapon, but he was willing to try.

The pilot considered briefly. There was still another jet fighter in the sky who would finish them in an instant if they showed any offensive intent. On the other hand, if they were going to crash anyway, they might as well take the Russian helicopter with them.

His optimistic side prevailed.

He made one more check ahead. Through the largest hole he thought he saw a darker area, a blotch on the still waters.

An island, he decided. He remembered from the charts he had studied before the mission.

"Hold your fire. I think there's an island ahead. I'll drop you guys there and see if I can get out during the confusion."

"An island?" Harris didn't approve. "How the hell are we going to get to the mainland?"

"Swim," the pilot said.

His choice evaporated anyway. The Russian chopper had taken up a position directly in front of him. And the last Mig was throttled back, making banking circles around the intruder.

"Bullshit," Shepard snarled from the intercom. "No islands."

"No choice."

The camouflaged helicopter shuddered as the cannon on the port side let loose a burst, aimed at the circling jet.

"No!" the pilot screamed. "For chrissakes—"

But it was too late. The other cannon was in action, too, and for a moment the jet climbed frantically, escaping disaster only because of the untrained men at the guns.

The remaining Russian—the helicopter—wrote the finale. In one burst it chipped away the ends of a rotor.

Shivering and quaking, the American chopper began losing altitude. It obviously wasn't going to make the island.

They were going down.

Chapter One

The new headquarters building for the guerrilla warfare school at Fort Bragg was a miniature Pentagon, a six-sided doughnut with a corridor running along the outside. The offices and conference rooms looked out on an atrium in the center. Shrubs and grass flourished there in the wet and moderate climate of North Carolina.

In the building's small theater the only light came from the exit signs and the reading lamp on the podium, where Mark Stone stood.

Seated before Stone, in the last row, was Terrance Loughlin, and two rows closer sat Hog Wiley. Carol Jenner sat in the first row on the right, next to the emergency exit.

Stone was a big man with the muscular coordination of a hungry tiger. He had been a master sergeant in a Green Beret Special Forces unit stationed out of Da Nang during the Vietnam War. His speciality had been covert actions of all kinds, usually involving hit-and-run, cross-border operations into Laos, Cambodia, and North Vietnam. He had undergone extensive stateside training in all of the classic infiltration techniques, including weapons, demolition, hand-to-hand combat, survival, paratroop training, and camouflage. He had played a vital part in some of the most sensitive operations of that war, and had the distinction of having served more tours of duty in Indochina than any other Special Forces soldier.

In the years since that dirty war Stone had begun returning periodically to Southeast Asia in search of living American missing in action prisoners of war on behalf of the families of such men. It was a matter of honor and nothing else.

Stone and his team had on numerous occasions isolated and penetrated P.O.W. slave camps, neutralizing resistance to rescue American prisoners. The catch had been that, until very recently, the more Stone had proved that there were living M.I.A.'s over there, the more intense had become the pressures to cease his unsanctioned activities.

The official U.S. government line was that there were no living M.I.A.'s in Southeast Asia, and Stone had first been branded a nuisance, then a maverick, and finally a criminal as he had moved increasingly outside the law. The C.I.A. had actually sent a team out after his head, and he and his men had become fugitives from federal indictments involving their M.I.A. work.

Until, yes, very recently.

Until a friendly senator had begun pushing for the powers that be to see the light. After much finagling, this had eventually resulted in no less than a presidential pardon for Stone, and an offer to broaden his scope of activities, operating decidedly off the record but with government sanction, utilizing the unique hard-punch capabilities honed to a fine edge by Stone and his men during their M.I.A. missions.

Based out of Fort Bragg, Stone's team would be brought into action whenever and wherever American military, government, or civilian personnel were declared "Missing in Action," around the world, when standard diplomatic or military response was inappropriate.

The way the world was going these days, it was thought such a team could and would be kept more than a little busy in global hotspots.

This was the first mission for Stone and company since the presidential pardons. Stone sensed the edginess of his teammates.

Loughlin and Wiley sat sideways in their seats, their hands subtly on the butts of their concealed weapons. They could gun down anyone entering the unlit auditorium.

Wiley's selection of a seat two rows closer to the front was not a random choice. Seated in the same back row, he and his teammate might kill each other if they opened fire on someone entering through the double doors in the rear wall.

Carol Jenner had the emergency exit covered.

This maverick team did not take chances. They had spent too many missions "in the cold," functioning on their own, treated as outlaws by their own government as much as any Communist country.

Terrance Loughlin was a former commando of the Special Air Services. He was big, rugged, and unflappable.

Hog Wiley was a huge, hairy, powerful asskicker from east Texas, unpolished and wholly without couth but a magnificent fighting man.

An attractive, sensitive woman in spite of her association with Stone's violent team, Carol Jenner had never touched a knitting needle in her life. Given her way, she would have been out in the field on every mission, but she was stuck stateside. Someone had to run the team's headquarters, and she was it.

There was one other woman in Stone's life: Rosalyn James, an army nurse who Stone had been in love with in Vietnam. One of Stone's last "outlaw" M.I.A. missions had been to return to Southeast Asia to rescue Rosalyn, who he'd long thought dead. During the war Stone and Rosalyn had talked of marrying when it was over, but anything like that was now on hold. Readjustment after so many years of captivity was a long, painful process. Stone knew enough to give Rosalyn all of the time and space she needed to heal. He was fully supportive of her and saw her regularly, but he understood and accepted her need to take whatever time necessary to get her head and her life back in working order after her long, terrible ordeal.

On the screen of the darkened theater were the enlarged file photos of two men, a front and side shot of each.

"Don Shepard and Jack Harris," Stone informed his team from behind the podium. "Company contract operatives and our mission objectives."

"Are those their real names?" Carol asked.

"Probably not. Twenty-four hours ago they left Honduras and were choppered into Nicaragua."

"Their mission?" Loughlin asked.

"To connect with Contra leaders in the countryside and assess their effectiveness."

"Sounds like fallout from the Iran-Contra arms fandango," Hog grunted.

Stone nodded. "The drop should've gone off without a hitch. It didn't, which is where we come in." He flicked on the theater lights and turned to a large map of Nicaragua tacked to the wall. "The chopper went down somewhere in this small area." He drew a circle in white chalk on the map, then a line and another circle. "This is where they were headed, only a few minutes away when the Sandinistas caught up with them."

"How y'all know that's where they went down?" Hog asked.

"Wreckage," Mark said. He tossed the chalk into a

box. "Intelligence says the two C.I.A. men have been turned over to Soviet interrogators at a secret mountain camp."

"Where's the camp?" Hog said.

"We don't know. That's a big chunk of the problem. The Reds keep secrets pretty good." He looked at Carol Jenner. "Carol is going to monitor the mission for us."

Loughlin said, "OK, they're in a secret camp, probably well-guarded, and all we have to do is get them out in the next three days, right?"

"Something like that."

Carol asked, "Why did the Sandinistas turn them over to the Soviets?"

"Possibly because the Communists don't trust the peasant government in Managua." Mark turned to the map. "As I see it, our best bet is to hit Managua and see if we can shake loose any info about where the Russians are holding our agents. The latest off-the-griddle info is that the two agents are in Managua or were. They may have already been taken to the secret camp. One man in Managua will know."

"El Presidente?" Loughlin guessed.

"Close," Stone said. "General Romero Perez, a big wheel in the military."

"Any scoop on where we can find Perez?"

Stone smiled. "The guy is flamboyant. Everyone in Managua knows where he lives. It's a big estate."

"Won't we need a letter of introduction?" Hog groused.

"We may need a bit more than that," Stone said dryly.

The media, and much of the American intelligence community, had not been told that a U.S. helicopter had been shot down in Nicaragua. U.S. aircraft were not supposed to overfly that country. The chopper had been on a secret mission and had run into bad luck or an

ambush or . . . And only a handful of people knew about
it.

The Oval Office did not want any hint of scandal
linking the C.I.A. with the Contra rebels. So, unfortunately, the longer the American agents were in enemy
hands, the worse it was—the more likely the story
would get out. The newspapers and the television news-
hawks loved that sort of thing. And, of course, the Russians were using the silence to their advantage.

Just how much the two captive C.I.A. men knew
about covert Central American operations, Stone had no
idea. But, with all the hullabaloo about the capture, it
was likely they knew enough to severely damage the
U.S. Intelligence posture if they were made to talk.
Years of work could go sliding down the drain.

Carol said, "Sounds like this first official M.I.A.
mission for Uncle Sam is going to be a real beaut."

"And me not even knowing Spanish," said Loughlin.
"Hell, I don't even know the word for 'women.'"

"You won't have time for women," Stone assured
him.

"Sounds like we ain't even gonna have time to take a
crap," Hog grumbled. "Uh, sorry, Carol, honey."

"Time is of the absolute essence," Stone told them.
"From here on out, it's one big countdown. Our gear is
packed and a C-130 will be lifting us off in fifteen minutes."

"Just enough time to make out my will," Loughlin
said grimly.

Chapter Two

The plane made a wide circle, losing altitude, and came in softly to land on a little jungle strip that was barely long enough to allow the big C-130 to set down. It was the middle of the afternoon and humid. The sky was blue with high streaky clouds, and they were in the middle of nowhere. Nowhere, Honduras.

The pilot swung her around expertly and taxied back to a crummy-looking cluster of huts and shacks beside the strip. He shut off the engines, and the plane seemed to settle down as if wanting to rest after the long trip.

In a moment the plane was surrounded by a chattering group of ragged soldiers and civilians, one of whom pushed his way to the front of the noisy crowd and faced Mark Stone as he came to the door. He was a short man, gathering fat about the middle, using a large handkerchief, which he patted his face and neck with. He had a gleaming smile.

"Welcome to Honduras, amigos," he said, with no trace of accent. "I am Emilio de la Torre at your service." He said, motioning, "Jump down and have a drink. The soldiers will take care of your baggage."

15

"Howdy, Emilio," Hog said, slapping the little man on the back. "You got any cold beer?"

"Well, sort of cold. Come on."

The soldiers hauled their gear from the plane and they followed De la Torre into one of the huts. This was apparently an ongoing operation, Stone thought. The soldiers were already unloading the big plane as if they were used to it and knew exactly what to do. Trucks were backed up and orders shouted.

In the hut De la Torre provided chairs. There was a small bar, and he set out bottles and glasses. "I am the C.I.C.," he told them. "The Civilian in Charge. I was told to expect you."

Hog selected a bottle and a glass. "You speak better English than I do."

The little man lifted thick brows. "I was raised in San Diego, U.S.A. You think I should speak Rumanian?"

Stone laughed and flopped in a chair with a full glass. Hog said, "What d'we do now, neighbor?"

"Now I take you to a hotel."

At their blank looks he explained. "There's a village just around the hill. It's called Rosal, after an early settler, I suppose. Anyway, the hotel is palatial for these parts. It has five rooms."

They laughed, and Loughlin asked, "Then what?"

"Then I introduce you to Captain Vega, and he'll take it from there. I'm finished." De la Torre spread his fat hands. "That's all they told me."

"How do we get there?"

"I brought my limo. Drink up and we'll take a ride."

The limo turned out to be a dark blue small-window VW beetle that was parked behind the shack. De la Torre said, "I call her Marianne. Let's pile your gear on top."

There was an aluminum frame bolted to the top. They strapped the gear on and squeezed into the little car, a tight fit for four big men. De la Torre's nose was an inch from the windshield, and the little car seemed to wince and groan with the weight.

When the C.I.C. started the engine, it clattered and protested, billowing smoke out the exhaust, shuddering, but finally settling down to a steady chatter. "She is obstinate sometimes," De la Torre said. "Like all women, you have to pamper her." He shifted into first and the car jerked, slowly gathering speed. He shifted into second. "She needs new plugs, I think. I have promised to get them for her. Maybe she doesn't believe me."

"Women are funny," Loughlin said, winking at Hog. "How far is the village?"

"About five miles." De la Torre glanced at them. "You must be very important hombres. You know you are getting our best red carpet treatment." He shifted into high.

"We're used to limo service," Stone said. "Marianne is first class."

"She's the best car in the area," De la Torre replied with a touch of pride, "not counting trucks. I didn't want to put you on one of them." He ducked his head, looking out at the sky. "It'll be dark in an hour or less. Be sure you eat at the hotel. The café is terrible."

"Thanks," Stone said.

The road was only a deep-rutted two-track path winding through pines and thick brush but generally level. It must be murder in the rainy season, Stone thought. They were at the bottom of the valley, with generous mountains on either side, and now and then he could glimpse the sheen of water off to the left; probably a stream. The little car bounced along, chugging furiously, with a plume of dark smoke trailing them. De la Torre needed rings as well as plugs.

The first shot came from almost dead ahead. It slammed into the front of the little car with a sound like a hammer hitting an anvil.

Instantly Stone grabbed the wheel, and Marianne bumped off the road and ran headlong into the brush as De la Torre yelped in terror.

The only too-familiar snarling, crackling of an AK-47 came from the direction of the stream, and bullets smashed the rear of the car, pulverizing it. Glass shattered as the rear and side windows went and bullets pounded through the roof, making the car jump and shudder.

Stone had rolled out, into the weeds, the .44 magnum in his big hand. He crawled forward away from the car and flattened out, eyes searching for enemies, the pistol extended.

Loughlin and Hog Wiley were out of the car in seconds, and Hog's Uzi spat at a target.

Stone fired at a muzzle flash—wham, wham, wham.

He rolled again, wishing it were darker so he could see the flashes better. How many did they face? And who the fuck were they? No one knew they were coming! Almost no one.

A fusillade came from the right, more bullets smashed the little VW, tearing part of the hood off, ripping the windshield to shreds.

Hog answered the fire, spraying the underbrush in that direction. Stone fired at another flash and rolled. He saw a figure rise and fall back. He had hit one of them—whoever they were.

Hog and Terry were moving apart. He heard Loughlin firing and crawled back to get around the shattered car. Most of the firing was coming from the right.

Bullets were hacking at trees, and leaves and twigs showered down. Stone emptied the magnum at another muzzle flash and rolled into a slight depression to reload. Bullets chewed the ground where he'd been. He wished he had a grenade or two, but they were still in the packs atop the car.

He heard Loughlin say, "I got two of the sonsof-
bitches. . . ."

Hog replied, "Keep your dumb head down."

Stone crawled around the car and into a patch of
ferns. Was the ambusher's fire slackening? They had put
at least four of them out of commission.

He saw a flitting form and snapped a shot. Another
figure jumped from one tree to another, and he fired
twice, seeing bark fly on the tree. They were retreating
all right. Another dark figure crossed his line of vision,
and he and Hog fired together.

The figure halted, as if he'd run into a wall, and
dropped into the weeds.

Loughlin said, "They're pulling out, chums."

Stone glanced toward the stream. No fire had come
from that quarter for several minutes. Hog was swearing. His Uzi got off a quick burst. Then silence.

An eerie silence. Were they waiting for a move? Or
were they gone?

Stone began to crawl forward slowly, the pistol
ready. In moments he came across a body. It was a man,
wrinkled and weather-beaten. He was dressed in ordinary cottons with a leather belt and holster. His pistol
lay several feet from his clawed fingers. His chest was a
red pulp. There was a battered Kalashnikov under him.

He heard Loughlin say, "They're gone. Like birds in
the fall, they've gone south." He was far over to the
right. "I can see a couple of 'em bugging out."

Stone got to his feet warily. He looked back at the
VW, wondering if De la Torre had gotten himself into a
hole.

Hog came from somewhere in front. "I made a quick
tour. They're gone all right. Left three behind, 'nother
one here."

"One over at the stream," Stone said.

"I figger they was about eight in all. Look like
farmers t'me, out pickin' on tourists."

Stone holstered the pistol and they went back to the car. De la Torre was crumpled beside it, his left side shredded. He had received a burst as he was getting out of the vehicle; he had no pulse.

"Damn," Stone growled.

"He was a pretty good guy," Loughlin said sadly. "Too bad."

"His number was up," Hog said philosophically. "Can't beat your number. This here beetle is a bust, too. Ain't five square inches with no bullet hole."

Loughlin walked across the road. He came back with an AK-47 over his shoulder. "One citizen there, smashed to jelly. These poor fuckers got a lot to learn."

"Learn what?"

"None of 'em knew how to lay a goddamn ambush." He leaned the AK against the car. "I guess we walk into town, huh?"

"I reckon."

"So who were these gents?" Stone asked. "Did they know we were coming? How could they know? The colonel is careful as hell about missions."

"You ast us, then you tell us the answers," Hog pointed out.

Stone growled, "It's a bad start. I hate like hell to get ambushed before I'm even on the job."

Hog flicked out a knife and cut the straps holding their gear on the aluminum frame. He looked it over, noting a few bullet holes. The attackers had been aiming at the car, not the packs. That was good of them. He piled the packs by the road. "What'll we do with all this here Russian artillery?"

"Leave it for Captain Vega, whoever he is," Stone said. He walked to the middle of the road and peered down it. The trucks should be loaded by now; they'd be coming along soon and give them a ride. Had they heard the battle?

Loughlin said, "I don't see how they could know we were coming."

"Unless they're goddamn good guessers," Hog put in. He wiped the Uzi lovingly. "I knew a gal once, back in Fort Worth, could work a Ouija board like you wouldn't believe. She could bring back yore Uncle Peanuts—"

Loughlin asked, "What the hell is a Ouija board?"

"Don't you know anything for crissakes? A Ouija board is a gimmick that tells the future. You call up somebody who's passed over—"

"Passed over what?"

"'Passed over' means they gone to that great barbecue in the sky."

Loughlin shook his head.

"Get your stuff together," Stone said. "The trucks're coming. We'll hitch a ride."

Captain Vega met the trucks in the center of the village. They pulled their packs off and piled them to one side, and the trucks went on. Vega gave them a snappy salute. Stone offered him a drink.

Vega was a smartly uniformed Honduran officer, a very polite heel-clicker. He was on duty at the moment, he said, and must not go into a public bar.

He was genuinely horrified to learn of the ambush and the death of De la Torre. He immediately strode across the street to where a group of soldiers waited and sent them, under a sergeant, to the spot.

"They will bring back the bodies," he said. "This is a terrible thing. Señor De la Torre was well known and liked. It is a great tragedy."

"We liked him, too," Loughlin said.

"I think these men must have been bandits. I regret to tell you we have them here. However, I am delighted they did not harm you."

They were standing in the street. Mark Stone said,

"Is there somewhere we can talk, Captain? A little more privately?"

Vega smiled. "Come with me, if you will, senores."

He led them into a two-story building and up a flight of stairs to a wide, almost vacant office. It had a desk and two rather frail-looking chairs and a bench against one wall. When they were inside, Vega closed and locked the door.

"I have certain orders," he said, looking from one to the other. "But of course I cannot help you officially." He stressed the *"officially."*

Hog and Loughlin lifted the bench and placed it near the desk. All three sat, and Vega rounded the desk and unfolded a map upon it. "This is a map of Nicaragua." He put a book on one corner, an inkwell on another, and leaned over it. "Where are you bound?"

Mark joined him and pointed to Managua. "How about there?"

"Ahhh." Vega nodded. "Very well. I can get you across the border safely and into the hands of some people who will guide you."

"What kind of people?"

"They call themselves freedom-fighters. They are peasants, but they know the terrain. They will pass you from one group to another till you reach Managua."

Loughlin asked, "How far can we trust them?"

The slim young captain shrugged. "I cannot tell you that. There is—how do you say it—bad fruit in every barrel."

"All fruits are bad," Loughlin said. "Of course, that's only an opinion."

Vega frowned at him. "I don't—"

"Don't pay any attention to him," Mark said quickly, giving Loughlin a look. "Tell us more about these guides."

"It is about a hundred and fifty miles to Managua as the crow—I believe it is the crow?"

"Yes."

"As the crow flies. But you will undoubtedly travel twice or three times that far because of the terrain."

Hog asked, "Why can't we go by chopper?"

Vega smiled politely. "Because our only aircraft is Honduran, and we cannot fly over Nicaragua."

"No private choppers?"

"None at all, to my knowledge, senores. I am afraid you must march."

Or steal a car, Mark thought. If there were roads. He frowned at the map. Nicaragua was a damned mountainous country, especially in the central part. Managua was on a lake, the smaller of two lakes. Too bad there wasn't a river going their way.

"I will take you in the morning to the border where you will meet Manuel. I will send a message to him tonight."

"Does he speak English?"

"Oh, yes. A great many people speak it or enough to understand. Manuel is not a young man, but he has lost all his family to the Sandinistas and has much reason to hate them. He knows every secret trail in this part of the land."

"Good," Stone said. "May we have the map?"

"It is yours, senores."

The only hotel in the village, as De la Torre had told them, was not much. It was called La Joya, the jewel, but was not. It did have a brave front—someone had painted it recently—but the foyer was dusty and showed its age, and it had only five rooms on two floors. One room was occupied. It did not seem a going concern.

It was run by a worried-looking man, his wife, and his teenage daughter, who did all the chores. The man, thin and stooped, was named Rutilio. He also had sev-

eral acres outside of the village that he farmed because
the hotel, which he had inherited, did not support them.

They signed for two rooms, using names made up on
the spur of the moment, and flipped coins to see who
would sleep where. Rutilio was delighted to have them,
rubbing his hands together, running to see that they had
threadbare towels.

The restaurant, a square tiled room, was run by a
large black woman who spoke no English at all but who
nodded and smiled at every word as if she did. The
menu contained only one item, tortillas and frijoles,
with raw sliced tomatoes, but they did not complain.
They werc the only customers, though Rutilio had told
them the restaurant was often crowded at midday. And
being *Norte Americanos,* they were eating much too
early for the native population. They sat around the
table in the large empty room with echoes bouncing
after every word, and after they had eaten, Captain Vega
showed up.

He had brought a bottle and poured drinks all
around. It was impossible, he told them, to say who
their attackers had been. There was nothing, not a scrap
on the bodies, to identify them. All their arms were
Russian made, not new and doubtless stolen, so Vega
supposed they were part of some irregular band, maybe
even guerrillas or bandits. He could not believe the men
had been paid to intercept them. He spread his hands
eloquently. "How would they know?"

Stone asked the pointed question. "Did *you* know we
were coming here?"

Vega shook his handsome head. "I did not, senores,
not until De la Torre told me. He had received a radio
message, he said. It was in code and did not mention
names. Three men would come this day. That was
all. . . . Of course, he was to aid them in whatever way
he could."

"Then De la Torre was more than just a civilian agent in a small village?"

"I believe so, senor. I must say that I am very annoyed this attack has come in my sector. I am sure they came across the border. . . ."

"You've had other raids?"

"Not for many months. It is the first in a long time. I have only sixty men here, and we must watch too many miles of border. My superiors call this a quiet sector. It may be that you were simply unlucky."

"Has there been much trouble along the border?"

"*Sí*, it comes and goes. It is very possible that you were attacked because you were in an automobile."

Stone nodded, reflecting that De la Torre had told them they were getting the red carpet treatment. In a poor country people who owned automobiles could be considered rich . . . fair game for banditry.

There had been such irregular bands in Indochina, men who would kill for a pair of shoes or less. Was this something the same?

The night was uneventful. They locked the doors to the rooms and did not bother with keeping watch. They were all light sleepers, with weapons at hand.

Chapter Three

Their transportation was a small and well-used Toyota truck, painted a dull green. They saw no one on the street as they drove out of the village, heading south with Vega at the wheel, the following morning. They followed a very poor road, barely a path that wound in and out between the hills, bouncing them generously. They met no one.

When the road petered out, Vega parked the car. "We will have to walk from here on."

Stone asked, "How far is the border?"

"A few miles." Vega shrugged. "Perhaps three."

"How will we know when we reach it? Is it marked?"

"*Sí*, there are markers at intervals. This is not a well-traveled road, as you will see presently. There is no fence at the border. There is no village close by in Nicaragua."

"Do the Nicaraguans patrol it?"

"*Sí*, but often by plane or helicopter."

Hog said, "What the hell did the world do before there was helicopters?"

"You could say that about Kleenex," Loughlin remarked.

"It don't shoot at you."

Stone said, "Let's move it."

As Vega had hinted, the land quickly became gullied and harsh. Some of the gullies ran toward the south, steep-sided and deep, and there was no way to get around them. The guide, Manuel, would be waiting on the Nicaraguan side.

They slipped and slid into the largest ravine and followed the agile Vega in single file, pushing through brush and ferns, climbing over boulders. It looked as if no one had ever, in the history of the earth, been this way before. He hoped Vega would not get lost.

In fifteen minutes Vega halted, hissing at them. They stood motionless as a lightplane droned past a thousand feet up. It disappeared into the haze far to their right, and Vega motioned them on.

It took an hour to traverse several miles. Then the rutted land gradually became forested. The gullies petered out into a rising plain, and as they entered the protecting trees they lost sight of the distant blue mountains.

After another half mile Vega halted and blew a whistle. Almost at once there was an answer from somewhere off to the left. Then, in a few moments, a short, very dark, coarsely dressed man walked toward them, holding his hand up in the universal peace sign. He was followed by two much younger men, each of whom held an AK-47 vaguely pointed in their direction. When they recognized Captain Vega, they slung the weapons over their backs.

"This is Manuel," Vega said in a pleased tone, embracing the older man. He introduced the three of them as Manuel nodded, looking at them curiously. The young men were Jose and Alberto. They merely nodded when their names were mentioned. They did not look as if they had ever smiled.

Manuel asked, "You go Managua?"

"Yes," Stone said. *"Sí."*

"Den we go now," Manuel said. He looked at the two young men. *"Vamos."* They turned immediately.

Stone shook hands with Captain Vega, thanking him. Hog and Loughlin did the same, and Vega gave them a smart salute. "May luck go with you, senores."

Manuel was already far ahead, not bothering to look around.

"He don't fool around," Hog said. "These jaspers ain't got no tea ceremony. Jus' get your ass in gear."

They hurried to catch up, in single file again, and for several hours they marched steadily, the pace never slackening over easy ground. Manuel and his two led them a winding course, generally south, that ate up the miles. He seldom glanced about to see if they were coming.

When they came to a stream, Manuel halted for a few moments, then went on, and in the middle of the morning he halted in a grove of trees, saying they would rest for half an hour. He did not look as if he needed it. He sat under a tree, took out a pipe, filled it, and began to smoke.

"He ain't much to look at," Hog confided softly to Stone, "but he's steel wire inside. I bet you that sombitch can walk us all into dust."

Stone nodded. "No bet." He had already noted that Manuel and his two young companions were keeping a sharper lookout than previously.

At his question Manuel said, "Sandinistas close by." He pointed with the pipe stem. "Dey have camp two, t'ree mile that way." He got up and stretched.

Stone asked, "What kind of a camp?"

"Dey patrol dis . . . dis . . ."

"District?"

"Sí, district. Got airplane, many truck . . ."

"Let's go kick 'em in the ass," Hog said.

To Stone's surprise Manuel broke out into cackling

laughter. He poked Hog's big arm. "You good man! Damn good man!"

Hog grinned. "Told you so."

"Hell's fire," Loughlin said, to whoever would listen, "that goddamn Texan takes up with everybody— old ladies, cats—never fails."

"Cats don't stand around shootin' off their mouths," Hog said complacently.

When Manuel led out again, he seemed much more wary; he walked slower and stopped often to listen. There was almost no wind to rustle the pines, and the air was clear and sharp. At one point he sent Jose to the left and Alberto ahead, and they waited till both returned, nodding to the old man.

They came to a wide area that had been burned over, and Manuel carefully skirted it, staying within the shelter of the trees. It would have saved them several miles of walking, but Manuel jabbed his finger upward with a glance at Stone. He feared aircraft.

In an hour, as if the old man had conjured it up, they heard the familiar beating sound of an approaching helicopter. Manuel shouted and hugged a tree, standing motionless. Stone and the others followed suit, and the chopper roared by, close overhead. Were the Sandinistas looking for something? No, the iron bird did not stop or circle; it kept on going out of sight and hearing.

"Much bird," Manuel said, circling his finger. "Many goddamn gun."

"Just a patrol," Loughlin said, "using up the bloody petrol."

They came to a road soon after, a two-track path that seemed well used. Stone touched Manuel's arm. "What are our chances of stealing a car?"

Manuel studied him for a moment. *"Mucho peligro.* Dangerous. Many *soldados."* He shook his head. "No will stop."

Mark frowned at the road. They could put up a barrier and damn well stop a car. Of course, if the soldiers saw a barrier, it would alert them, and if they had a radio, they'd call for backup . . . and that might mean choppers. Gunships.

But what if they put up a barrier on a hairpin curve —if there were such a thing on the road. Then the driver would never see it till he was on top of it. Then there'd be a chance to knock them off. He drew such a curve in the dirt for Manuel, but the old man shook his head again. There was none close by.

But there was a village not far ahead. Manuel held up his hand with fingers widespread. *"Cinco kilómetros."*

"Five clicks," Loughlin said.

The old man sent one of the young men ahead as a scout. They stayed off the road, in the tree shelter, moving slowly, and Manuel constantly scanned the sky.

"He don't trust them choppers worth a goddamn," Hog said.

The old man looked back at them. "No talk." He put his hand behind his ear in an obvious gesture.

"Gotcha," whispered Hog.

They walked slowly for another mile, then Manuel halted suddenly, both arms out to the side. Mark cocked his ear. Was that a shot from up ahead?

In the next moment he heard a burst of automatic fire. Loughlin said, "Jesus!"

Manuel moved away from the road, motioning them to follow. He pulled the Kalashnikov off his shoulder and chambered a round. The other young man unslung his weapon and started forward but halted at a sharp word from Manuel. They exchanged rapid Spanish, then the younger, Jose, turned and ran to the left.

Several bursts of firing came from ahead, coming closer, and suddenly Alberto appeared, running hard. He shouted something to Manuel as he approached, and the older man instantly motioned and trotted to the left, calling to them, "Sandinistas!"

There was a wide downslope heavily forested; it was impossible to see more than a dozen yards in any direction. A few stray shots sang overhead but came nowhere near them. Stone jogged easily. The ground began to turn upward very gradually, and he could hear sounds of the pursuit. How many? It sounded like a platoon.

In another moment they came to a field, brown grass and weeds, and the ground sloped up steeply for a dozen feet. At the top, looking to Stone like nothing more than a row of jagged teeth, were rocks. An outcropping of rocks had been thrust upward ages ago in some forgotten earthquake. Manuel scrambled over it and turned, laying his rifle in a crevice pointing back.

It was a natural breastwork. "This good place," Manuel called.

Stone agreed. "Scatter out. If they come, we'll make them think we're a regiment." He turned to the old man. "How many Sandinistas?"

Manuel spoke quickly to Alberto and turned back. "He say maybe twenty."

Stone peered over the outcropping. The government troops had been fired on by Alberto and would be wild to chase him down, probably to execute him on the spot. They wouldn't know that Alberto had friends with him. It would be a deadly surprise. He noted that Manuel sent Jose to the left and Alberto to the right. They would signal if the enemy tried to flank them.

The outcropping was a strong position. They should be able to stop a charge of only twenty men—if it came. He moved along behind the jumbled rocks. But they should not tarry here too long. If the enemy ran into heavy return fire, they'd call for help. They'd know they were up against force and would want choppers to even things out. Not good.

He paused and looked through a crevice toward the oncoming Sandinistas, seeing no one. Where the hell were they? *Did* they know how many rifles were behind the outcropping?

Minutes passed and the silence grew. Stone looked at the old man, who was complacently chewing his pipe stem. He saw Stone's look and shrugged lightly. "Dey come."

Stone looked behind them; more forest and hills. Was this what Manuel intended, fire and fall back, fire and fall back? It could take days. Looking at the old man, he began to realize that Manuel wanted a crack at his enemies—now that he had support. Manuel had no urgency about him. To the old man, this was a private war.

Stone swore under his breath. They could not allow themselves to get embroiled in a prolonged hit-and-run battle. He halted by the burly Texan.

Hog said, "I can hear 'em flounderin' around out there. What if I discourage them a little bit?"

"Don't waste ammo." Stone peered between the rocks. "You see a target?"

"I see a feller now, a-stickin' his nosy head up." Hog squinted over the sights of the AK and squeezed off two shots, then chortled. "Right between the goddamn eyes."

They both ducked as a burst of automatic fire smashed into the outcropping, spraying them with bits of rock and dust. "Touchy bastards," Hog commented.

"We oughta keep 'em out of grenade range!" Loughlin called.

Stone agreed. "Don't let 'em get into the field. They can't throw from the trees. Try some ranging shots. Let 'em know there's more than one of us."

Loughlin fired a burst. Manuel opened up a dozen yards away.

Sudden automatic fire pounded the outcropping, ricocheting off the rocks and screaming into the air. For several moments it was a furious fire, seeking every crevice, raising dust. But doing no harm at all.

Loughlin answered with a burst, then ducked down, grinning. A hailstorm of high-velocity lead smashed and tore at the rocks.

Stone found a crevice and sprayed the undergrowth along the line of trees. All along the line they were firing and ducking, moving, and firing again.

The enemy was keeping up a steady fire, though much of it seemed unaimed. They must've known they couldn't punch through solid rock with bullets. . . .

Stone looked toward Manuel. Were the Sandinistas keeping up the fire while half of them moved around to the flank? In a moment he saw Alberto come in and speak to the old man.

At once Manuel beckoned to him, and Stone nodded. The enemy *was* flanking them. Manuel called, "We go dis way." He pointed to the left.

Loughlin led, behind Manuel, and they moved quickly with Alberto far out ahead of Manuel and Jose behind Stone. In moments the outcropping was far in the rear, still pounded by the enemy's fire.

Alberto went, straight as an arrow, through the trees, setting a hard pace.

In a few minutes the firing behind them stopped. Maybe the flanking party had discovered the defenders had gone. Probably. Now they would pursue.

Stone swore again; they were heading east rather than south. Each step took them farther from Managua.

There was a quick burst of fire from somewhere ahead and bullets rapped into trees nearby. He saw Manuel fall to the earth, motioning them down. The goddamn Sandinistas must have gotten ahead of them some way—or it was another force altogether. Shit!

Manuel was crawling to the left again. Stone heard Hog say, "Somebody done run into somebody else."

Stone crawled left and was surprised to hear an engine start up. They must be near a road. Another burst of fire came from somewhere ahead of him. The engine roared and two grenades exploded, one after the other in quick succession.

Loughlin said, "What the fuck is going on?"

A machine gun began firing from the direction of the road, bullets cutting through the trees waist high. When it stopped firing, Manuel got up and ran left, motioning them.

The machine gun opened up again, firing behind them, and they heard the engine. The gun was probably on a car, maybe even an armored car. Maybe the people in the car had glimpsed Alberto and fired at him. . . .

The ground became rutted, and they ran into more outcroppings. This must be a volcanic area, Stone thought. Nicaragua was lousy with volcanoes.

Manuel was just ahead of him, glancing back and motioning left. The firing stopped and the silence was eerie.

Then Stone heard a whistle and a chorus of yells, sounding like fifteen men, and they were running, firing as they came—heading for a spot about forty yards to his right. Stone rolled onto his stomach and leveled the AK rifle, cradling it.

To his left Hog said, "They're doin' a mighty dumb thing."

A soldier came into view, and Stone fired a long burst.

His bullets turned the man and smashed him, knocking him into the weeds. A second man, beyond him, tumbled.

Hog and Loughlin were firing long bursts, and the machine gun opened up suddenly, and bullets slammed into trees and cut just above them.

The charge was cut to pieces. Someone was moaning in the brush. The whistle sounded again, this time obviously a recall.

The firing stopped. Stone reloaded hastily, peering toward the enemy.

Loughlin said, in his drawling voice, "Think they had enough, mates?"

Manuel said urgently, "Dis way—*dese prisa!* Hurry!" He moved to the left.

Hog said, with satisfaction, "Got me three or four of them fuckheads. Imagine them buggers comin' at us that way, like they's on parade!"

"Shut up and follow Manuel," Stone said. "You can count your scalps later."

Loughlin growled, "Like to get me a shot at that fucker with the MG."

The old man led them directly away from the enemy. The Sandinistas must be raging, Stone thought. They had lost at least six men in the stupid charge. Hog was right, it had been a stupid move.

They were leaving a plain trail, as he could see glancing back. But nothing could be done about that now. A single shot came rapping into a tree only a foot from his head, and Stone ducked. He was the last in line; Jose had moved to his right. Peering at the back-trail, he could see no one.

He turned, and in a moment another shot came, sizzling past his ear.

Stone flopped on the ground, pulling the .44 magnum. He pushed it out, holding it with both hands, waiting.

A shadow moved, maybe fifty yards away, then moved again. He took up the trigger slack.

The shadow turned into a man carrying a rifle.

Stone's pistol fired and recoiled. The man jerked, crumpled, the rifle flying from his grasp. He disappeared in the undergrowth.

Jumping up, Stone ran after the others.

* * *

They were in a broad, shallow stream, walking single file toward the right with Alberto and Jose out ahead. It was an old leatherstocking trick, wading in a stream to conceal footprints. But it might work. At least their pursuers would lose a bit of time trying to decide if they'd gone upstream or down. Time was important.

In half an hour Manuel stepped out of the water onto solid rock, motioning them to follow in his tracks. They were in a valley, close by one side, a very steep brush-covered slope.

The ground under their feet was very rocky, and the immediate area held few trees and almost no cover. When they left the stream, they were in the open.

Stone frowned at the old man's back. Where the hell was he taking them?

And then he heard the beating sound of a helicopter, approaching *fast*.

Chapter Four

Stone glanced up at the chopper—two choppers! They were perhaps a mile away, making a gradual turn. The pilots had not yet seen them. They were doubtless in radio contact with the ground force that was tracking them.

Manuel shouted, *"Prisa, prisa!* Hurry!" He pushed aside the brush. The two scouts ducked under his arm and disappeared.

"Jesus! It must be a goddamn cave!" Hog said, running.

Stone made up his mind. Maybe the old man knew what he was doing after all. He ran toward the others. A cave was better than the shelter of a few trees.

Manuel ducked, seeing him approach, and Stone dashed into the brush—and was suddenly in a huge cave. The entrance was very small, but the cave was easily fifteen feet high and nearly round. And as he looked at it he realized what it was—a lava tube.

Years ago he had seen them in Hawaii and California. They were to be found everywhere volcanoes erupted. Obviously this one had been kept secret from the Sandinistas.

Manuel motioned. "We go—" He set out into the dark tube with a candle that had been waiting in a wooden box by the entrance.

"What'll they think of next?" Loughlin said, wonderingly. "It looks like it was made by a goddamn worm . . . a real big worm."

"A lava worm," Mark said. "Red-hot lava gouged this out."

"Just for us," Hog said admiringly. "I ain't got a bad thing t'say about lava from now on. Saved our butts."

So this was what old Manuel had been heading for from the first. Captain Vega had said they could trust him, and Vega had been proved right. He *had* saved their butts. If the gunships had caught them in a crossfire in a box canyon—that would have been all she wrote for sure.

The tube curved to the right, a long, gentle curve. It had a sandy bottom and, in the flickering light of the candle, rugged sides from which water dripped here and there. It was cold, and the farther they walked into it, the colder it got. In half a mile they were all shivering.

"Goddam," Hog said, "I would'n mind if a little of that lava showed up t'take the chill off."

"I don't believe this place," Loughlin said. "We got nothing like it in Britain."

"How many volcanoes you got in Britain, neighbor?"

"Damn few," the Brit growled. "Volcanoes aren't civilized."

"Well, this one's damn friendly," Hog said. "I'm declaring this here volcano a honorary Texan, so you watch what you say, amigo."

Loughlin rolled his eyes. "Honorary Texan . . . Jesus!"

They came to a place where the earth had fallen and where another tube joined. With only one tiny source of light they took forever to crawl over the clumps of earth and stones and reach a sandy bottom again. The tube bent sharply to the right and seemed smaller than the other. It was also wetter—the floor was damp and there were puddles here and there. But Manuel never faltered. "Come, come . . ."

The two young scouts ran ahead, apparently able to see in the pitch black.

It took another hour to come to the end of the tube. It was concealed as the other had been, mostly by boulders and brush. They came out into a forest. Manuel led them straight for several miles before halting on a ridge. The two scouts reported to him and disappeared again like wraiths.

Manuel said, "No Sandinistas close. We eat now."

"All *right!*" Hog bellowed.

Major Pedro Rosas was commandant of the Duodécimo, the 12th Battalion. He was a round little man with a red face and almost no hair. He had achieved his position through a dedication to Marxism—he had been to Moscow—and an equal dedication to those in very high places. It was said of him in secret that his big nose was very brown.

But now he was furious. He had received a report that one of his patrols had been fired on by an irregular group, and had allowed that group to escape capture after killing nine of his men. They had found no enemy bodies.

"How can this be!" he stormed at his staff. "Bring me the leader of this patrol!"

"He is dead," they told him. "He was cut in two by Kalashnikov bullets. They steal our weapons and use them against us."

"You are all idiots!" he screamed at them. "Send out more patrols! Where are our helicopters?" He ordered them out of his office and almost cried. What a terrible report to send to his superiors! They would ask him if he could not manage his district better—and what kind of a question was that? It had only one answer: He would crush all opposition or he would be replaced. There was no in-between.

When he calmed down, he sent for Lieutenant Paco Suran. Paco was a Nicaraguan, one of the enlightened ones who knew the trend of the world, a Marxist, and a man with ice in his veins.

It took an hour to find him and bring him to the commandant's office in greasy fatigues. He had been cleaning weapons, he said, and Rosas waved that aside.

"I am putting you in charge of finding the irregular group who killed nine of our companions and comrades. You will start at once. Select what men you wish, as many as you wish. All I ask is that you bring me proof of their deaths or the persons themselves. Do you have any questions?"

"No, Major."

"I will expect reports daily by radio." He waved the lieutenant out.

Paco immediately called Sergeant Salvador Cortes to his quarters. As he stripped off the greasy clothes he gave the other his orders. "You will pick twenty men. I want no malingerers—I can trust you for that. Arm them properly, rations for at least eight days. Bring along a map case, flashlights, matches..." Paco motioned. "Put them in two BTR-60's with ammo and radios. I want them ready in an hour. Questions?"

"No, sir."

"Then wear out your socks."

Cortes saluted and ran.

Paco then called for the NCO's who had been on the patrol, ordering them to his quarters. He showered and dressed and came out to find one man, a corporal, waiting for him.

"I am the only surviving NCO, sir," the man said.

Paco lit a cigarette and sat, frowning at the man. "Tell me what happened."

"We flushed a campesino—armed, sir—out of a village, and he led us to the group."

"A group of what?"

"Devils, Lieutenant. They fought like devils. We never got close to them—and they disappeared from under our noses!"

The man began to sweat as Paco stared at him. "They disappeared? How is that possible? You had helicopter assistance!"

"Yes, sir. But it's true all the same."

"They disappeared without a trace?"

"Without a trace, sir."

Paco snubbed out the cigarette and stood. "Get out of here, Corporal."

He paced the floor, lighting another cigarette. What the man had said didn't make sense—though the man obviously had not lied, probably hadn't the brains to lie. Something had happened, but what? It was possible the corporal was a fool.

Well, he must get on with it. He crushed out the cigarette, strapped on a pistol, grabbed his cap, and went out to the personnel carriers.

Stone walked behind Manuel when they left the ridge behind and came to a region of tilled fields surrounded by forest, with blue mountains on the horizon. In the shelter of the trees Manuel pointed. "Village dere, one, two *kilómetros.*"

It was a calm, peaceful scene, Stone thought. Shading his eyes, he could see a dozen or more workers in the furrows, all distant, some plowing with animals. The sky was a blue bowl with high golden and fleecy clouds as the afternoon waned. War seemed far away.

"Purty as the ass-end of a Saigon hooker," Hog commented, picking his teeth with a fingernail.

"Me, I like the tit-end better," Loughlin said. "Specially when they wiggle 'em."

"You figure asses don't wiggle?"

"Oh, I like an ass-wiggle, too, but there's nothing like a pair of tits . . . maybe with a little whipped cream on the nipples."

"Goddamn pervert," Hog said.

Stone laughed. "For crissakes. Will you two shut up?" He shook his head and followed Manuel along just inside the edge of the trees. He noticed that the old man had become very wary. He sent Alberto and Jose far ahead and constantly scanned the skies. He glanced back at Stone. "Many Sandinistas 'ere. Be much careful."

He halted once, holding up his hand, standing motionless as a small biplane droned across the blue, several thousand feet up. When it disappeared, they went on.

Loughlin asked, "Don't the rebels have any airplanes?"

Manuel shrugged.

As they approached the village Manuel led them deeper into the forest. In a while Alberto appeared and held a short meeting with the old man. Then he took off again.

Manuel turned. "Sandinistas in village." He shook his head. *"Malo.* Very bad. Shoot two people. Goddamn bad."

"Why'd they shoot them?"

"Alberto say *información."* Manuel made a face. "People no talk." He pointed his finger. "Boom, boom." He sighed deeply. "Very bad."

As darkness fell they went around the village, giving it a wide berth. They could hear music, wafting across the fields, as somebody played a radio. As the stars came out they crossed a cornfield, walking between the rows of rustling stalks to gain the forest again.

"Reminds me of home," Hog said. " 'Ceptin' I don't hear no coyotes."

They had come a long way toward Managua, Stone thought, as he consulted the map, but they had a long way yet to go. They made camp in a ravine with towering pines on every side. Hog pushed stones together and made a fire in a low spot, and they broiled meat and made coffee.

When they had finished eating, Manuel said he would have to leave them the following day. He had come to the edge of the area he knew well. He was unfamiliar with the territory ahead.

But he had a cousin in a village only a dozen miles distant. His name was Romiro, a good, honest man and a foe of the government. He would be their guide. He knew every pine tree and rock by their first names and knew exactly how to avoid the hated Sandinistas. Manuel assured them he would speak to Romiro himself.

In the morning they ate cold breakfasts except for coffee, and as they were getting their gear together for the march, several choppers appeared a few miles to the east and seemed to be searching. As far as they could tell, the choppers were quartering the ground.

"Probably looking for us," Stone said.

"Yeh," Hog agreed. "We'uns is probably famous in certain circles."

Those distant planes were almost their undoing. They had claimed the interest of the little group and lulled them into thinking they were safe because of the distance. But as soon as they started out, a gunship strafed them. It came roaring in at treetop level with guns blazing.

An irrigation ditch was all that saved them. They piled into it, a five-foot deep, badly dug ditch with sheer sides. Manuel dived into it headfirst with the rest of them toppling like ninepins to escape the pounding shells. The two scouts were a mile ahead. Mark yelled, "Scatter—get as far apart as you can!"

The ditch was not straight, or they might have been

in big trouble. The gunship pilot tried desperately to shoot down the length of the ditch but could not.

They dodged from side to side and took advantage of every fold and crease. And when one of them was safe from attack, he fired at the chopper. These distractions possibly saved them as much as anything else. Mark saw pieces of the chopper fly off now and then, and finally the pilot gave up a bad job before he was blasted out of the sky.

They watched him swing about and head south, gaining altitude.

And they knew he was using his radio to tell where they were. They were pinpointed exactly.

"How'd he know it was us?" Hog demanded.

"He didn't, but he saw armed men where there shouldn't be." Mark shook his head. "We were god-damn careless, and goddamn lucky. Let's just pray to all the better class of gods that the luck holds out."

Manuel stopped the chatter. "We go," he said.

They went quickly, jogging through the trees toward the village. Manuel was sure there was a highway only a few miles to their right. Soldiers might even now be piling into trucks to bring them here.

The village was tiny, squatting in a wide valley with cultivated fields surrounding it on three sides. The fourth side was hilly and forested. They holed up there while Manuel walked alone into the village, trudging along like a campesino. The two young scouts left their weapons behind and followed him, each carrying a load of wood for disguise.

He was gone more than an hour. Long shadows were stretching across the land when he returned alone. He had bad news. His cousin, Romiro, had died a month ago.

Hog said, "We's screwed, neighbors."

Mark said, "Is there no one else?" They would be lost without a guide.

Manuel shrugged. "A man offers. He is called Raul."

Mark said, "Do you know him?"

"No, senor. But he is the only one."

"And he knows this country well?"

Manuel shrugged again. "One hopes."

Loughlin sighed. "That's a hell of a reference, one hopes. Why can't we go on just using the map?"

"We could, in peacetime," Mark said. "There'd be buses running, too."

"I vote we get that jasper," Hog said. "Looks like he's better'n nothing."

"Hell's fire," the Brit said, "a hooker with the clap is better'n nothing."

"So you vote no?" Stone demanded.

Loughlin made a face. "All right. He blew out his breath. "Count me in."

There were about forty Sandinista *soldados* stationed in the village, Manuel told them, but it had been easy to avoid them.

Stone said, "Don't take any chances."

"*Sí*, senor." Manuel walked back into the village in the gathering dark. He was gone a short time and returned with a slim young man he introduced as Raul.

Raul was about thirty, Stone thought. He was slight and black-haired with a thin mustache and pipe-stem arms. He had been a schoolteacher in Managua, he told them, and wished he were back there. But he had lost the job because it became known to the authorities that he had talked against the government. He had been severely warned, and had come home to his village and was now working in the fields.

"Can you guide us to Managua?"

Raul smiled. "*Sí*, of course." He had family there, he told them, and would like to visit them and do the government a bad turn at the same time.

Stone was eager to get away, but Raul had to return

home to get a pack. He had not known, he said, that they wished to travel at once.

There was nothing to do but wait while he went back into the village.

Manuel said his good-byes. "I will stay tonight in the village. . . ." He wished them all success, and Hog embraced him.

"Y'all done good, little neighbor. You watch yore backtrail."

Loughlin grasped Manuel's hand. "I think Hog just made you an honorary Texan."

Chapter Five

To Lieutenant Paco Suran the radio was an extremely important tool. He received reports of every freedom-fighter or Contra clash in northwest Nicaragua. It was difficult to sift among them to decide which was the group he sought . . . if any.

But when the report came to him of a single helicopter battle with a group of armed men, he set out at once with his two personnel carriers for that location. The helicopter pilot had received severe arm and chest wounds in the clash and had broken off the engagement to fly back to his base for treatment. There were also forty-three bullet holes in his machine.

The pilot had jotted down the coordinates, and when Paco arrived it was impossible to tell where the irregulars had gone. However, he had marked on his map the location of the battle where the group had first been noticed. And a line drawn on the map from that location to this, pointed generally south. The strange band of armed men was moving south. Why? Who were they?

He ordered his carriers to head south. Probably they were on a mission to join with a stronger force of Contras. It was an educated guess. For the time being he would have to react and counterpunch. But there would come a time when he would set a trap and haul them in. Paco Suran had no doubts at all.

Raul was gone more than an hour. Two helicopters appeared in the dusk and landed on the far side of the village where several bonfires were lit, possibly to light a landing zone.

When he finally came, with a pack strapped to his back, Raul was full of apologies. He had not known that he would be going on an extended journey, and he had much to do in a very short time.

"Troops will be searching for us in the morning," Mark said. "Lead us to an area where we can escape an air search."

Raul nodded. "We will go this way, then." He led them across a fallow field and into a long, narrow valley that took them mostly west.

As they got well into it Hog fell back to march beside Mark. "Don't like this much, amigo. We get spotted by a gunship in this here twat-shaped valley, we's got troubles."

Mark was thinking the same thing. Militarily speaking, it could hardly be worse. But then, who would expect a schoolteacher to be an expert on tactics or terrain?

Loughlin felt the same way. "Makes me nervous."

Partway through the valley Mark made a decision. The mountain range to their left was rugged and forested but not at all impassable. He halted them. "We'll go south from here," he announced, noting the grins from Hog and the Briton. Raul looked suddenly shocked. "But this is the closest way!"

"Closest way to Hell," Loughlin said, drawling the words.

Raul looked at him. "What do you mean?"

"No more talk," Mark said. "Move out." He pointed. "Hog, take the point."

Raul said no more, but Mark heard him grumbling to himself. He was probably muttering that they were fools to hire a guide and not let him do his job.

Hog set a hard pace and they followed, strung out in single file with Mark bringing up the rear. As they began to climb, Hog halted in a copse of skinny pines and suddenly motioned them down. Mark fell prone, hearing the engine of a small plane high above them. It passed and he got up, scanning the sky. Had the pilot seen them?

Hog led them a roundabout way, staying in the shelter of the largest trees. They saw no more planes and three hours later they crossed the ridge and started down the south side . . . and halted. Hog yelled at Mark, "Why not go along the ridge?"

Mark nodded. As he took the first step he heard the drone of an engine. "Down!"

He dropped, seeing Loughlin pull Raul down. A small plane passed over them several thousand feet up and continued on. They would have been hard to see through the thick covering of trees, Mark thought, watching the plane disappear in the mists. But why so many planes all of a sudden?

They moved along the ridge for an hour or two. Hog stayed well in front as point. In late morning they came up to him. He was draped over a boulder, prone, using binoculars pointed into the valley they had left earlier.

He gave the glasses to Mark. "Somethin' moving down there. See what you figger."

Mark focused the binocs carefully. The narrow valley had closed in. There had been a gigantic landslide in some primeval time, leaving the face of the mountain pale stone where nothing grew. The floor of the valley was largely filled with rubble; only a tiny pathway seemed to wind among the earth and rocks.

And beyond the landslide were trucks and milling men, a hundred or more at a quick estimate.

He handed the binoculars to Loughlin, glancing at Raul. Hog was fingering the butt of his pistol. "Soldiers down there," Mark said in a conversational tone to Raul.

"I know knothing about it!" Raul said, looking from one to the other of them.

"How come they're there, then?" Hog asked. "Y'all the only one knew we was coming this here way."

"I told no one! Not even my wife!"

Loughlin said, "They're setting up an ambush, looks like." He smiled at Raul. "I'd say they expect us down there."

Raul was wringing his thin hands. There were tears in his eyes. "I told no one! I swear it! It has to be a coincidence! Maybe they had some other information!"

Terry patted his cheek. "If we really thought you did it, we'd cut your balls off. *Comprende?*"

"All right," Mark said. "We give him the benefit of the doubt." He moved close to Raul and patted him down. "No gun. No knife. Let's move out."

Paco received word that an ambush was being set up in the valley, turned his carriers around, and headed there at once. The message center could tell him only that word had been received that an irregular band would be traveling the valley. It was apparently an anonymous tip. He was familiar with them.

Was this the group he sought? There were any number of small rebel bands, some bandits, roaming the countryside, taking advantage of the unrest and war. He asked the message center to radio the ambushers not to kill the approaching band, but to capture as many as possible, even though he knew his request would probably be ignored.

The roads were terrible, but his BTR-60's were

eight-wheeled vehicles with a top speed of 50 MPH, and he could expect an average of 30 MPH over a long period. They reached the ambush site, after a long, roundabout route, at dusk. The troop commander, a slim, buglike major, was very unhappy. Their prey had not come through the valley—nothing had been sighted but a lone goat—and he was out of sorts and wanted no conversation with a suddenly appearing lieutenant.

"Did you send out scouts?" Paco asked.

"We sent out every fucking thing but the cook!" the major yelled. "It was a bad tip."

Paco got out, feeling frustrated. Obviously the stupid major had made elemental mistakes, and the outlaw band had detected him and his men. He drove to the nearest village for food and drink and to pore over his maps.

Maybe Major Rosas was wrong. Maybe there was no particular band—his men might have been killed by bandits who had long since scattered to the winds. He ordered another drink.

Stone took the point, and they went down the mountain into a wide and gullied valley where a stream wandered like a lost soul. It was an excellent place for cover, but they made poor time. There was a road winding through the valley, but they were loath to use it until Loughlin said, "It's a gamble. We'll make half the time pushing through the sticks, and anyway, we'll hear a vehicle long before it reaches us, right?"

Hog was of the same opinion. "Lemme git out in front. I got ears like a eagle."

Mark said to Raul, "Is there a village in this valley?"

"No, senor."

Mark motioned Hog to take the point, and they went on much faster for more than two hours. It was early afternoon when he stopped, and when they came up to him, he was smiling.

"What is it?" Mark asked.

"There's a truck around the next bend, an old Chevy."

"Soldiers?"

"No more'n five. I seen five anyways. If there's six, he's out taking a crap."

"What'd they stop for?"

"One of 'em's made a fire. I guess they drinkin' coffee or havin' a bite."

"We need that truck worse'n they do," Loughlin said. He checked his Uzi. Hog did the same.

Raul was horrified. "You're going to kill them!?"

Hog was astonished. "Hell, no. We goin' send them a card askin' for the loan of it. Ain't that the civilized way?"

Mark pointed to Raul. "You sit right here. If you run off, we'll find you."

"An' paddle your ass," Hog promised.

White-faced, Raul sat down in the grass. He was shivering as they moved out.

Loughlin went wide to the right, off the road into the gullies. They would give him ten minutes to get into position. Mark followed Hog around the bend. Halfway around they went to their bellies and crawled, coming to a stop in clumps of brush beside the road.

It was an old Chevy, dark blue with yellow designs painted on the hood. Some unknown artist had indulged himself. The truck had been pulled off the road into a flat area under some age-old cedars. Four men were sitting around a small fire, talking and laughing. The fifth man had walked down the road and was gazing off toward the distant mountains.

Mark watched the second hand of his watch race around the dial. In two minutes Loughlin would be in his spot. He crawled half a dozen feet from Hog and pushed the big .44 through the brush. He didn't care for executions, but—

The fifth man suddenly shouted and began running back to the truck. "What the fuck—" Hog said.

There was a burst of fire from the right, and the man stumbled and went down, arms flailing. He hit the dirt and plowed into it with his nose and was still.

He must have spotted Loughlin . . . or a metal reflection. The four men around the fire reacted quickly.

Mark squeezed the trigger and watched his victim hurled backward, legs flopping limply.

Hog's Uzi chattered viciously and another man whirled around and fell.

A third pulled a revolver and fired once toward them, but a burst from Loughlin cut him almost in two.

The fourth man made it to the truck. He snatched an AK from somewhere and turned, firing it full auto. Hog's Uzi and Mark's .44 magnum smashed him to pulp. The Kalashnikov stitched a row of holes along the side of the mountain and fell from lifeless fingers.

It was suddenly silent.

Remembering Hog's statement that five were all he saw, Mark remained still, searching the area with his eyes. Nothing moved but the leaves of the trees. Loughlin came in from the boonies, his gun ready, eyes darting here and there.

"I think we got 'em all," he said.

Mark rose, holstering the pistol after reloading. They pulled the bodies aside, dragging them by the heels. The truck had an open body and contained sleeping bags, four assault rifles, canteens, food, and shovels. There were also five boxes of thirty-round detachable rifle magazines. A good haul.

"We've gotta bury these guys," Mark said, "and police the area. They never existed."

It took an hour or more to dig a trench to contain all five. They put it out in the field away from the road, and when the bodies were in and the hole filled, they spread grass and weeds on it till it looked like the surrounding area.

"Who was it said war is hell?" Loughlin asked, leaning on a shovel.

"It was me," Hog replied. "I say that ever' now and then. I think I even wrote it somewheres."

Stone rummaged in the truck and came up with an unlabeled bottle that turned out to be brandy. It was only half full. They passed it around, then flung the empty into the weeds. They were getting ready to depart before Stone remembered Raul. He walked around the bend to find the schoolteacher still sitting there, head pillowed on his arms. He looked up when Stone yelled and got slowly to his feet.

"Let's go. Get the lead out." He was one hellova soldier, Stone thought. A full-blooded rabbit. Poor guy.

According to the gauge, the truck had plenty of gas and the tires were fair. "With a little luck," Stone said, "it ought to get us to Managua."

They spread the map on the hood. "Where the hell are we?"

With Raul's help they were able to make an educated guess. They were farther north than they wanted to be, and maybe halfway to the capital. But Raul was positive the road they were on would take them nowhere. Only a few decent roads crossed the mountains, and there were plenty of mountains to cross before they reached Managua.

This road, he told them, would peter out soon. It probably only connected a few villages and farms. They would doubtless come across a highway later on.

"What we need," Hog said with unassailable logic, "is a airplane, a chopper, or a fuckin' balloon."

They folded the map and walked up the road a bit, away from Raul. "You think that bugger is shittin' us?" Hog demanded.

"About the road?"

"About the road and ever'thing else. I wouldn't trust him any farther than I could throw a forty-pound turnip."

"Well, why not let him walk back home, then?" Loughlin suggested.

Stone rubbed his chin. "If you're right and he *is* a wrongo, and we let him go, won't he put the constabulary on our trail chop, chop?"

"Yeh." Loughlin nodded. "If he really is a Sandinista deep down, he knows too much about us."

Hog grinned at them. "Y'all wanta make damn sure? Let me take him over in the woods a minute. I'll find out, or he won't piss green no more."

Stone said, "We only suspect him . . . on pretty lousy evidence. The guy could be straight, up and up and square."

"All right," Loughlin said, snapping his fingers. "We give him the benefit of the doubt."

"Hog?" Stone asked.

The burly Texan nodded. "OK. Saved by the bell. But he makes a wrong move and I kick his ass up between his ears."

"You're all heart," Stone said.

Chapter Six

The truck was easy to start and ran well, though it gave out a lot of black smoke. Probably needed a ring job, Hog thought. It had no radio and showed 98,000 miles, but the counter had gone around twice from the look of the truck. The seats had obviously been replaced many times, and the dashboard was a welter of dents from boots.

Mark drove with Hog beside him, the Uzi across his knees. Terry sat on a sleeping bag in the back with Raul, and for the first twenty miles they saw no one. However, the road got worse and worse, and they had to move slower and slower and frequently get out to move large rocks out of the way.

It was a pain in the ass, as Hog said a number of times.

But the road got better a mile or two from the village. Mark halted instantly as soon as they spotted it. Raul thought it was called La Cruz, but he had never been there. The village was a mile or so distant, with smoke rising from home fires. There was a fringe of trees about it and open fields to the left. They could see the gleam of water reflected in the late sun.

Mark said, "The road goes through the village. What d'we do—abandon the truck and go around it, or go see if there're bad guys waiting for us?"

"A recon is called for, chum," Loughlin said. "We wait for dark and slide in to have a look."

"Anybody have a better idea?"

"Let me go," Raul said. "They won't give me a second look, but they will know you are *Norte Americanos* in an instant."

They looked at each other. Then Mark gave them a wink when Raul was not looking. "Ok," he said. "You go in, Raul. We'll wait here by the truck. But no funny stuff."

"Funny stuff?"

"No tricks."

Raul looked offended. "I will not trick you." He glanced at the sky. "I will return as soon as possible . . . after it is dark."

"Why not right away?"

"Because if there are Sandinistas there, they will be suspicious if I go and leave so soon. I must be cautious."

"All right," Mark said. "Do it your way. We don't want any suspicion. We'll bed down and wait."

Raul nodded and started toward the village. He glanced back once to see them all sitting and lying in the grass by the truck. But as soon as he was out of sight, Mark led them off to the right, in a circle around the village.

With infinite care they crept close to the house in the gathering dark. From a vantage point in one of the last shacks, Mark spotted three trucks parked in the center of the village. That could mean thirty or forty men. Two of the trucks had tall aerials sticking up and each was armed with heavy machine guns, their ugly snouts thrust out over the cabs. The distance was too great to tell what they were, probably Russian made. A guard with a slung rifle lounged against a fender and lit a cigarette.

There was no one else on the streets except a couple of dogs. Maybe the people were frightened by the presence of soldiers and were staying indoors.

As he watched, Stone saw three soldiers go to one of the trucks, and one man climbed into it and put on headphones. Stone nudged Hog. "They're using the radio."

"You figger that little shitface, Raul, told them about us and they reportin' it?"

Stone sighed. "It could be."

Loughlin said, "Let's go sit where we can watch the truck. If those soldiers go and surround it, then we can be sure Raul is a fink. Right?"

"He's a fink all right," said Hog. "When a shithead looks like one and smells like one, chances is, he *is* one."

They faded back into the line of trees and retraced their steps to a position where they could watch the truck without being seen.

They had only a short wait until a group of about twenty men came out of the village, formed a line, and closed in on the truck with rifles ready. In a moment they saw flashlights playing over it, then a couple of men got into the cab and drove it back into the village. The men on foot followed.

"That settles it," Stone said. "He gave us up."

Hog scratched his chin, watching the truck disappear in the gloom. "Wonder iffen I could find out where he's sleepin' tonight. Maybe I could—"

"Forget it," Stone said. "We've gotta be miles from here before morning. They'll surround this area and use Bill Bailey's fine-tooth comb. Let's head south."

They moved into the dark, and Loughlin remarked, "He knew we were heading for Managua, chums."

"But not what for."

Hog said, "Them fellers got our truck, and they got two others in the street there. Maybe we c'n steal one and—"

"If we steal one, they'll know exactly where we are," Stone retorted. "On that road. Every chopper in Nicaragua will be breathing down our necks in the morning. Besides, the road may only go a mile or two, and all the trouble'd be for nothing."

"We shoulda booby-trapped that truck," Hog said morosely. He grunted. "I guess all this easy livin' must be makin' me soft."

"That must be it," Stone agreed.

Loughlin said, "I hate to let that little prick outsmart us. I sure hope we see him again."

"He didn't outsmart us, he just ordinary double-crossed us. And we half expected it, right? Let's get to a place where we can throw a flashlight on the map."

They walked into the forest, toward the west, for half an hour and halted in a ravine. Mark spread the map on the ground, and they studied it by the light of a flash. Mark circled La Cruz with a pencil. "There's mountains all around and all this part of the country is forested. That's our only hope. I'm sure they'll try to find us from the air—depending on how bad they want us. So when we hear engines, we freeze. They'll be looking for movement."

Loughlin said, "How about if we travel at night?"

"Too slow. We'll make twice as much time by day. We have to take the chance. We also have to be miles from here by morning."

Hog said, "Let's go west, then. We c'n bend south later."

"That gets my vote," Mark said. He looked at the Brit, who nodded.

* * *

They halted as daylight crept over the land. They were on high ground, following just below a jagged ridge heading, by Mark's compass, generally southwest. Hog, out in front as point, found a small, scooped-out hollow and made a tiny fire in it for coffee. The smoke lost itself in the tall trees around them. They could see nothing but mountains and trees; they seemed to be alone on the planet.

Until the first helicopter appeared.

It was several miles away, following a distant valley. It disappeared into the mists, and Hog said, "They're lookin' for us, neighbors."

"Persistent buggers," Loughlin observed. "They could get on a man's nerves."

They continued along just below the ridge for several hours, halting once to let a plane soar overhead. No pilot had a chance of spotting them. The ridge divided and they went west till it finally began to flatten out.

Using the binoculars, Mark could see the country ahead was farmland. It was a wide plateau that vanished into mists with distance.

The chopper caught them in the open.

Some trick of acoustics or ground kept them from hearing it till it was almost atop them, coming from behind at treetop level. It roared overhead and opened up with machine guns as they scattered.

Mark rolled onto his back, slamming shots with the .44 magnum, hearing Hog and Loughlin's Uzis stuttering. He saw the chopper swing wide suddenly, taking evasive action, and thought he saw glass smashed.

He reloaded the pistol and slung the AK assault rifle off his back. It fired rifle rounds instead of pistol and was very accurate. He led the chopper and squeezed off two, three, four rounds, certain he was hitting.

The pilot jinked and swooped and his shots were going wild.

When the plane came nearer, Hog switched to auto and emptied the magazine into the ship as it raced over him. He saw black smoke curl from it and yelled, "He's hit, the fucker is hit!"

Mark slammed in a new magazine and rose to his knees. The chopper was quickly out of range, and he watched it disappear.

"He's hit bad," Loughlin said. "The sonofabitch picked off more'n he could chew." He reloaded deftly. "We got us a chopper, mates."

"And he knows where we are," Mark pointed. "Let's backtrack. They'll expect us to keep going, huh?"

Hog said suddenly, "You bleedin', son?" He picked at Mark's fatigues. There was a bullet hole in the sleeve. The slug had gone through without touching him. He hadn't even felt it.

"The devil's grabbin' at yore ass," Hog said. "You better change yore habits."

"Since you're so goddamn cozy with him, you tell him t'go fuck himself."

Hog laughed. "He's probably the only one c'n do that, too."

They retraced their steps quickly, expecting more choppers any moment, but none came. Regaining the high ground, Mark used the binoculars, scanning carefully in all directions, seeing no movement at all. Damn curious.

Loughlin mused, "Maybe we hit his radio."

That seemed the most likely. The chopper would have to return to base before an alarm could go out.

Lieutenant Paco Suran raced to La Cruz with his two carriers when the radio report came in. A campesino had escaped from the three men holding him, three dangerous *Norte Americanos* who had killed five men to steal a truck. Paco was positive this was the group he wanted.

When he stood before the slim schoolteacher, he *knew* it. "Where are they headed?"

"To Managua, senor."

"Why?"

Raul shrugged. "I do not know, senor. They did not tell me."

"Can you guess?"

Raul shook his head. "How could I guess?"

"You were with them, idiot! What were they like?"

"They are all very big men, very dangerous, very quick. I was in fear of my life every second."

"They wanted you to guide them?"

"Yes, senor."

Paco tapped his chin thoughtfully. "So they do not know the country." He stared at Raul. "What did they talk about?"

"Women."

Paco made a rude gesture. "Everyone talks about women! What else?"

"About stealing an airplane."

Paco sighed. "There are only three men?"

"Yes, senor."

"They haved killed fourteen men that I know about. . . ."

"They are devils, senor."

Pace frowned at him. "So am I."

He got rid of the quaking little schoolteacher. The man could tell him nothing. He got out his maps and spread them on a table, and, with Sergeant Cortes, he discussed routes. Which way were the *Norte Americanos* likely to go? Raul had hinted that the group was in a hurry, that they had discussed stealing an airplane . . . that suggested hurry. So why would they not continue toward the south?

Sergeant Cortes thought they might go west, to confuse the pursuit, but Paco overruled that idea. The men they sought were in a hurry—they would go south.

They hurried out to the personnel carriers and sped off in that direction.

As Paco left the village a helicopter was seen to crash only a few miles away, leaving a great column of black smoke. When an officer and a squad of ten men arrived on the scene, there was little to see but burning wreckage. Some of the metal parts of the chopper had obvious bullet holes.

The officer made his report: The helicopter had met an enemy in an unknown location, and the pilot had been seriously hit and had tried to bring his plane in but had crashed. The pilot was unfortunately dead.

There was apparently no activity in the wide valley below them to the south.

Mark said, "Let's cross it now. Maybe we can beat the pursuit."

"Leave 'em diddlin' around in our dust," Hog agreed.

They were halfway down the mountain when a column of trucks appeared. Apparently there was a road and they hadn't seen it. As the column passed, the last truck halted, and they watched ten men hop out and make camp. In a short time there were several fires and men were making coffee and cooking food.

"Sonofabitch!" Loughlin said. "Will you look at that? What the hell are they doing!"

"Exactly what we don't want," Mark said disgustedly. "That helicopter pilot must have told them after all. . . ."

"Or somebody is lucky," Hog said. "Somebody is pattin' Lady Luck's ass more'n we are."

"Well, we got to get across that valley. We'll just have to go around them." He looked at the sky. "It's too long until dark—"

Loughlin took the binoculars and examined the camp. "They're in a bloody good position on high ground so they can see in both directions." He looked toward the right. "There's another truck about half a mile down."

"Diversion," Stone said. "We need a diversion. Somebody think of something."

The big Texan smiled. "That grass out there looks dry. What about fire?" He wet his finger and held it up. "Wind's blowin' to the east. Mebbe we c'n find us a gully or arroyo and set us a right nice fire. Smoke them jaspers out."

"They'll know who set it," Loughlin protested.

Wiley laughed. "With a fire lickin' at their asses . . . ?"

"It's worth trying," Mark said. "Move out. Let's find a gulley upwind. We'll set the fire and keep going."

They moved to the right and came down slowly to the valley floor, stopping at intervals to use the binocs, keeping track of the men around the truck. One man was standing on the truck bed, obviously a lookout, and when he turned their way, they froze in position.

The floor of the valley had looked smooth and level from the mountain heights, but when they finally reached near it, they could see it was rugged and gullied with huge tangles of grass and leafed vines. It was land totally unsuited for grazing or farming, probably the reason it was uninhabited. But Hog was sure he could set it afire.

"They's plenty of dry stuff underneath them green leaves."

"You're sure?"

"Ain't this the dry season? That'll burn like Mama's cookin'."

Loughlin said, "Who's got a better idea?"

No one had. "Maybe the Lady is smiling at us," Stone said hopefully.

"Pat her ass," Hog said. "She likes it when you kind of roll your hand around."

"C'mon, let's do it." Stone got down on hands and knees.

They crawled along a gully for a quarter of a mile to get opposite the parked truck. The car was off the road on high ground, and as they came near, they could see that it would be almost impossible to cross the road without being seen by the lookout.

They separated to light the fires.

Hog was right, there was lots of dry grass matted close to the ground, and it took fire quickly and smoke curled up, spreading out—and the lookout saw it almost at once.

They heard him yell, then shots came smashing along the gully.

Stone yelled, "Get across the road—" He scuttled along after Loughlin, coughing when the smoke swirled around and enveloped him. There was one hell of a lot of smoke, and he cursed it at first, then realized it was helping to hide them.

The fires they'd set burned fiercely, eating into the undergrowth, making their own wind, which swept down on the truck.

The firing stopped, and Stone could hear the truck engine. Someone was driving it away, probably afraid the fire would reach it.

He reached the road and ran across it. Hog and Loughlin were there, coughing and swearing but grinning at him. Hog said, "Ain't that some fire, neighbor? You want a fire, you call ol' Hog."

"Get moving," Stone growled, and Hog waved and continued crawling along the gully, heading for the trees.

The fickle wind suddenly blew the smoke away from them, and Stone ducked low. The guy in the truck was

firing a large caliber machine gun, tearing up the rim of
the gully, showering him with dirt. Sonofabitch!

Stone found a niche and lay on his belly with the .44
magnum. He tried one shot, but the truck was too far
away. He pulled the AK off his shoulder and shoved the
muzzle through the niche. The lookout on the cab was
pounding shots farther along; apparently he had
glimpsed Hog or Loughlin.

Squeezing the trigger, Stone fired short bursts at the
machine gunner, seeing metal ripped off the cab—then
the gunner threw up his hands and disappeared. The gun
pointed at the sky.

"Gotcha," Stone said aloud. Jumping up, he ran hard
along the gully. He had a glimpse of another man
climbing onto the truck bed, swinging the gun around.
Stone flopped as the first shells began to land.

Hog was lying prone, aiming shots at the guy—then
the truck began to move. Hog fired a long burst at the
gunner, knocked him off the cab, and turned the AK on
the truck engine. Another burst halted the truck, then
the rifle clicked empty.

Stone caught sight of the second truck. It was start-
ing to move toward them. He yelled at Hog. "Get the
fuck out or we'll be caught between two of them!"

Loughlin was far up, almost to the trees. He began
firing and they hurried along the gully. It seemed ten
miles to the trees and a few bursts from the trucks were
pounding the rim, tossing dirt and rocks about.

Loughlin was yelling something at them and pointing.

Stone looked up to see a gunship bearing down on
them.

Chapter Seven

Their clothes were the color of the earth and the valley was layered in smoke, so the chopper didn't pick them up at once. Loughlin threw AK rounds at it, smashing a Plexiglas panel, and it swooped and climbed as if in a hurry.

Hog lay on his back and squeezed off single rounds at it, and the helicopter made a series of rapid turns. Stone thought it looked clumsily handled; they could discount it for the moment.

One of the trucks was approaching, the cab gunner pouring a stream of lead toward them. Much of it went over—the gunner evidently could not see them and was firing by guesswork. Terry Loughlin turned his attention to the truck, pounding at the front tires, and it suddenly swerved and came to a halt.

Stone poked Hog. "Now move, *move!*" He could see men pouring from the truck, at least ten of them, running into the field. He hurried after Hog as bullets began to crack overhead.

The gulley became wider and deeper, curving toward the west, with rocks and ferns lining the bottom. Turning, Stone emptied the AK magazine at the approaching

men, thirty rounds, and they scattered like quail, yelling. He saw two knocked down and thought he had hit
two others.

He slammed another magazine into the rifle as the
chopper passed overhead, giving him an excellent shot
at its belly. He stitched a row of holes and it suddenly
swerved, rocked crazily, then pulled away, losing altitude. Stone's jaw gritted; maybe he had hit the pilot.

Turning, he ran hard, jumping over boulders. He was
around the bend, out of sight of the pursuers on foot . . .
for the moment. Hog was far ahead and his Uzi stuttered. He was hunched over, firing to the right. As
Stone approached he sent a burst through the tall grass,
swore, and ducked as a salvo of 5.56 slugs ripped and
tore at the edge of the ditch.

"They're tryin' to flank us," he growled at Stone.
Then he yelled and pointed. Stone turned in time to see
the chopper flip up and land beyond the stalled truck,
rotors smashing, with several tossed into the air. A sudden gust of flame and a huge cloud of smoke rose, and
they heard the distant explosion.

Stone grinned. "I got me a chopper!"

"Count yore scalps later," Hog said. "Let's get the
fuck outa here."

"Right." They ran down the curving gulley as a grenade exploded some distance behind them.

Somebody was anxious.

The gulley made a sharper turn to the left, and Stone
halted, waiting till the first few pursuers came into
sight. He sent half a dozen aimed shots at them—the
fools were bunched up.

Three were knocked down; the others pulled back
hastily.

A small plane was making circles high above them,
well out of range. It might be too high up to see much.

The line of trees was close now. And the ground
began to slant upward. The gulley was petering out on

the edge of a landslide area. Small new trees and clumps of grass grew on the uprooted earth. Loughlin was there, lying between two clumps, firing quick bursts, sniping at the pursuers with deadly precision.

Stone watched Hog take up a position several yards on the other side of Loughlin. He switched to the AK rifle and began to potshot the men from the truck. Not many rounds were coming their way now. Stone crawled between the grass clumps, getting his breath.

He turned about and laid the AK in a convenient crevice; this was a hell of a good position. They were higher than the valley floor and could look down on the attackers. Good old high ground. Always grab the high ground.

He was a dozen yards from Loughlin and Hog. The chopper was burning in the field, the black smoke drifting off to the north. Men were working at both trucks, half a mile away at least. He could see very little movement in the gulley. The leader should call them off if he had any brains. They were all through for today.

Loughlin called, "I think the little fuckers have had it." He made his voice very British. "Anyone for tea?"

"Tea an' grits," Hog said.

The attackers were withdrawing. Loughlin was right; they seemed to have had enough. They must have suffered nearly a dozen casualties, with maybe one of the trucks put out of operation, to say nothing of the dead chopper.

"Let's git," Stone said. "They'll have an army here in two hours."

Hog led the way with both the AK and the Uzi slung over his back. They went up the mountain, following game tracks when they could, stopping now and then to blow and rest. Two choppers were over the valley, circling, and as they watched, one landed.

They could not see, even with the binoculars, that a large body of men had arrived to pursue them. Undoubt-

edly the Sandinistas would like to corral them, but they
probably could not spare very many troops just to capture a few men. It might be the sole reason they were
still at large. Of course, the land was wild and they were
the needle in the haystack.

They made the ridge by nightfall, tired to death. And
while it was still light Wiley found a small cabin hidden
in a draw. It was possibly a poacher's cabin and had not
been used for a long time. But it had a tiny fireplace, no
windows, and a plank door on leather hinges. They
made a fire and cooked the dried meat they'd brought
along, and after eating they kept the fire going. It was
cold so far up the mountain.

In the morning Loughlin walked back to the ridge
with the binocs to look at the valley—and discovered
that men were coming up the mountain. They were far
down—trudging along in single file, well out of range
of his AK-47.

He ran back to the hut and routed them out. Hog
insisted on booby-trapping the hut with a grenade, tying
the pin so it would be pulled out when someone opened
the door.

They filed down the mountain on one of the many
shoulders, brushing out tracks for several hundred
yards. The route down was not difficult and brought
them out onto a level plain partly forested and partly in
corn and beans. There was a village off to the right and
a road that disappeared into the distance.

They went to the left, into a forested area, and immediately hit the ground, hearing engines. Five trucks and
a jeep went by them on the road, not a quarter of a mile
distant.

Mark said, "I think they're Contras." Hog confirmed
it, peering through the glasses.

They saw no one else the rest of the day and, after a
rest in the evening, moved to the road and continued the
march till the lights of a village came into view. They

left the road then and circled through the fields to come up to the village from the side. It was a tiny place, straddling the dusty road, and there were no vehicles in sight.

Low hills loomed up to the west of the village, and they retreated to them, finding a place to bed down but posting watches. Hog was on watch near midnight and woke Mark, shaking his shoulder.

"What is it?"

"There's a Russki armored car in the village. One of them old six-wheelers."

"How d'you know?"

Hog grinned in the night. "I went over and looked at it. Heard it come in."

Mark sat up. "An armored car..." He smiled. "How many other vehicles?"

"None. That's it. Watched 'em dump petrol into it, then they posted two guards."

"How many of them altogether?"

"I only seen four."

Loughlin woke at the sound of their whispers. "What're you yakking about?"

"Russki armored car in the village."

Loughlin smiled. "We *need* an armored car. "What is it?"

"One of them six-wheelers."

Loughlin nodded. "Probably a BA-10. They made about a million of 'em. It's got two 7.62 machine guns."

Mark asked, "Can you drive it?"

"I drove one in Britain years ago. It belonged to the Imperial War Museum. Think I can remember..." He reached for his AK. "The one I drove had a 45mm gun too."

"Let's go," Mark said. "Lead out, Hog. Show us the car."

They went across the dark fields to the village, walk-

ing softly, weapons ready. The car crew had undoubtedly stopped for the night and would not move out till at
least dawn. As they reached the first houses Hog
stopped and went to one knee. Mark came up beside
him and looked into the shadowy street. One of the
guards was walking slowly toward them, a cigarette in
his mouth, a rifle slung over his shoulder. He looked
anything but alert.

Hog whispered, "Other one's in the car."

Mark whispered back, "Let's take this one out."

Hog nodded.

The guard stopped near them, opposite the last
house, and stared into the countryside, finishing the cigarette. Hog rose silently, drew his Walther pistol, took
four steps, and brought the barrel down on the man's
head. The guard fell like a stone, and Hog caught him
and dragged him off the street.

There was no outcry from the armored car.

Quickly Mark put on the guard's cap, slung the
man's rifle over his shoulder, and stepped out to the
street. Hog and Loughlin would circle the village and
meet him at the car. He imitated the guard's slow pace
and started back toward the car. It would take him five
minutes to reach it.

He drew the .44 magnum and held it down at his side
so that no one in front could see it. Where were the rest
of the armored car crew? Doubtless in one of the buildings opposite where the car had halted. But which one?
Probably they would soon find out.

As he approached the car he could easily make out
the guard's head and shoulders. The man did not move;
he might be dozing. But as Mark came closer he
stretched and said in Spanish, "It is time to change? . . ."

Mark grunted. The man was too far to reach. He'd
have to go around the other side of the car. He started
around the back of the car, and two men came out of the

house on the car's right. Mark halted; they had not seen him. Where the hell were Hog and Loughlin?

The three men of the car's crew were talking as the guard stepped out—then one of them noticed him, and Mark saw the man's eyes widen.

The man went for his pistol.

Mark brought the .44 up and the shot blasted the night.

Hog's Uzi spat bullets and two men were down—but the third ran back into the house, shouting in Spanish.

Mark yelled to Loughlin, "Start the car." He followed the crewman into the house. It was pitch black inside. He heard Hog say, "I'll go around. . . ." Then he heard a smashing sound.

Damn, he wished he had a flashlight. Someone screamed to his right, a woman's voice. And then Hog yelled, "He's out here!"

Mark went back to the street. Loughlin had the car's engine running. He grinned from the driver's seat. In a moment Hog appeared, shaking his head. "Sombitch got out through a window and run into the field. Too fuckin' dark."

"Let 'im go. Let's get the hell outa here." They piled in, and Loughlin put the car in gear.

Dawn found them miles from the village on a dirt road with a dust cloud following. They seemed to be moving through a jungle that threatened to close in on them any moment. It was the dry season, *verano,* or the road would have been a quagmire. The heat was oppressive, and in the first fifteen miles after daybreak they were fired on twice. One burst went over and single shots hit the rear of the car, doing no damage.

"We're targets for any rebel with a gun," Stone said. "They think we're government guys. Let's hope they're lousy shots. Keep your heads down."

They pulled over under the trees and consulted the

map. They could only guess where they were. The map did not delineate the small back-country roads and villages. It was almost useless. As Hog said, "With this here map and a good match you could start a fire anywhere."

They made coffee and checked weapons, distributing ammo among them. Loughlin asked, "How big is this country, anyway?"

"You could lose it anywheres in Texas," Hog said, yawning.

Stone folded up the map. "I read somewhere it's about the size of Louisiana."

"Wasn't there a lot of talk about putting a canal across it? I mean, instead of in Panama?"

Stone shrugged. "Yeh. Don't know what happened to that idea. It'd be a hellova ditch, I guess." He stretched. "Shall we bug out?"

With Loughlin driving, they came around a curve just before midday and found three big trucks in the road before them. Men were sprawled under roadside trees, obviously taking a noontime break.

"Don't stop," Stone growled. "Steady as she goes. They'll think we're one of them—until the last minute."

An officer walked casually into the road with his hand up.

"Give 'er the gun!" Hog yelled.

Loughlin pushed the pedal to the floor, speeding up. The officer yelled and jumped back in alarm. There was barely room to pass the trucks, half on the road and half on the rutted shoulder.

The car skidded and swerved, gaining the road again as someone fired into the air. The sprawled men suddenly came to life, scattering as Hog and Stone fired short bursts to get their attention.

An assault rifle sprayed them with bullets that spanged off the side of the car and ricocheted away.

Stone fired at the truck engines but could not see if the fire took effect. In seconds they were past, careening down the road.

But men ran into the roadway, kneeling to fire after them, and for a moment bullets ripped and slashed the air and rapped into the hull.

The heavy six-wheeler rocked and skidded, but Loughlin fought it and managed to keep it under control, shouting that some of the slugs had hit the rear tires.

Then, as they rounded a curve, the firing stopped.

"Sheeeit," Hog said, changing magazines. "They didn't even have scouts out. What the fuck kinda army they got anyways?"

"We got troubles," Loughlin growled, struggling with the wheel. The car was slowing, the rear end bumping and clattering. Both rear tires were shredded, flinging off chunks of rubber.

Loughlin stopped in another mile, shaking his head in disgust. "If they chase us with those lorries, we're sitting ducks, chums."

"We can't outrun them?"

"Hell, no. This heap wouldn't outrun a one-legged chicken. I can hardly hold it on the goddamn road."

Mark sighed. "Then we'll have to abandon it." He glanced around. "Where's those petrol cans?"

"Right here," Hog said. He pulled one from a metal holder and unscrewed the cap. As they jumped from the car he poured the gasoline over the interior, climbed out, and poured the rest over the engine.

Loughlin tossed a match and the car went up like a Fourth of July rocket. It became a huge orange torch, crackling and roaring as it consumed the vehicle.

It was still burning as they looked back from half a mile away. With the binocs they could see the trucks arriving, spilling men. But the armored car was finished.

And pursuit was sure. They were leaving a trail—it could not be helped. And after an hour's march, as they moved along a rounded hill, Mark halted them. "Why don't we try an old Indian trick?"

"What's that?" Hog asked. "Smoke a peace pipe?"

"Nothing that clever. Why don't we split up, each man go a different way... let 'em decide what to do then."

"And meet later somewhere?"

"Right."

Loughlin protested, "We'll lose firepower—in case we need it. In a good position we can stand off forty of those guys."

"Yes, while they radio for choppers."

Hog said, "Where'll we meet later? We don't know this country."

"We can all circle back to the road where we burned the armored car. We know where that is. We were heading southwest, so when each of us reaches the road again, he goes southwest. Sooner or later we'll join up."

"I don't like it," Loughlin said.

"One man leaves fewer tracks than three," Hog said. "We might just disappear into thin air."

"All right, but I still don't like it."

"Let's move out," Stone said.

Chapter Eight

When Major Rosas received the radio report concerning the stolen armored car, he went into a rage, throwing things and screaming. He shouted for his staff to find Paco Suran and haul him to headquarters to be skinned alive.

The staff scattered, sending wires, radioing, using the telephone, but no one could reach Paco. He was somewhere in the field; that was all Rosas could learn. And Paco's radio was out.

The radio was out because Paco's radioman was a cousin of a sergeant in the major's message center. At the first scream from Rosas, the sergeant had contacted Paco: "Get off the air and stay off."

Paco received messages but could not transmit. Until the major cooled down.

However, Paco went at once to the village where the armored car had been captured. Soldiers were still there, under a corporal, and Paco was told that three men had been killed by automatic fire; a fourth man had gotten away, and he reported that half a dozen rebels had attacked them as they were changing guard.

Paco had the man brought to him, a skinny, ragged-

looking specimen, nervous and jumpy. Paco said nothing for a moment, walking around the man, silently ex-
amining him from every angle. Was he lying? Paco
thought so. Half a dozen rebels? Very likely. It had to be
the three *Norte Americanos. They* would know how to
drive an armored car. The average campesino could
only drive an ox.

Paco barked to the man, "You say you actually saw
six rebels?"

The man trembled. He cleared his throat and hesi-
tated. "I—I thought—I, um, thought I saw them, sir."

Paco shoved his face close to the other's. "How
many did you see?"

"I—I saw. . ." The man hung his head.

"Go on!"

"I—I saw—one, sir."

Paco grunted. He stepped back, glaring at the man.
"So you saw one. Tell me about it."

"We—were changing the guard, sir. These men—
there must have been many, sir! They came from nowhere. I heard many voices."

"They came from nowhere?" Paco rocked on his
heels. "They were born without mothers? Is that what
you are saying?" He slapped the man's face. "Tell me!"

The man shivered. "I—I mean—they were suddenly
there, sir . . . firing at us. I was lucky to get away. I
don't know how I got away!"

"I see," Paco said sarcastically. "Some men dropped
from the skies and fired at you—so you ran."

The man said nothing.

"Well—is that all?"

In a very small voice, "Yes, sir."

"Get out." Paco motioned. The man hurried to the
door and paused. He turned, looking at Paco.

Paco lit a cigarette, puffed and examined some
papers, and deigned to notice the man. Finally, "Well?"

"There was one thing, sir."

"What?"

"The rebels—they shouted to each other in English."

Paco smiled. He waved the man out, nodding.

So it *was* the same gang of *Norte Americanos!* But *Cristo!* Now they had an armored car! He had to report it—because he knew the report would get to Major Rosas anyway. And he knew the storm it would arouse.

He strode up and down the hut, slapping his leg in annoyance. What would the damned *Americanos* do next? With an armored car mounting several machine guns they could shoot up every truck and jeep they met and cause immense damage. Rosas would probably try to charge him with every centavo of it.

He went out to the carriers and motioned. He would go south, too. If they stayed in the armored car, he should easily be able to trace them...and sooner or later he would overtake them.

Very soon he ran into the three trucks that were lined up along the road with guards posted. Just beyond the trucks was the armored car in a ditch, burned and still smoking. He could see at a glance that it was a total loss.

A sergeant told him that forty men were in the hills, chasing the criminals who had stolen the armored car.

Paco gazed at the car, paced up and down the dusty road, and considered his next move. What he knew about the *Norte Americanos* convinced him that forty men moving about the undergrowth on the hills were far too few to effect a capture. The man in charge, whoever he was, had made a foolish mistake. He should have brought in more men, surrounded the area, and used choppers to flush them out.

The fugitives had been heading for Managua. Why not go there and intercept them? As it was, he seemed always to be a jump or two behind and might never catch up. The *Americanos* were damned resourceful and dangerous.

But—on the other hand, there were dozens of ways
to get into the city, and he could not hope to watch but a
few. No, that course was impossible. If they once got
into the city . . . He shrugged. He was reduced to following.

He went back to the carriers and got out a map, calling Sergeant Cortes to look. Where would the fugitives
go next? The sergeant was sure they could continue generally south, since their progress, as Paco had recorded
it on the map, had shown no great deviation.

Also, south of the jumbled hills now being searched
was a highway that led to Managua. Paco was certain
the *Americanos* were heading for it, and Cortes had to
agree. It seemed logical.

So, Paco decided, instead of joining the search in the
hills, he and his men would travel as quickly as possible
to that highway.

And lie in wait for their prey.

Stone took the middle route when they split up.
Hog went to the right, Loughlin to the left.

The pursuers were close behind them.

The hills were a jungle with patches of tall grass
everywhere and forward progress was slow. Especially
if one tried to leave no trail.

Stone moved into the undergrowth at a crawl, looking for a place to hole up. It was difficult to see three
feet ahead.

He could hear the men coming up the hill, slashing
with bayonets, talking. They were coming very slowly,
forcing their way through the tropical growth, swearing. . . .

Mark smiled, feeling more confident every moment.
The jungle was advantageous to the pursued. His
clothes were almost camouflage enough, but he found a
depression and covered himself with leaves and grass
and lay still.

The soldiers were grumbling among themselves as they passed by him. They well knew the reputations of the men they were after and none wanted to face them alone. Out of sight of their officers, they bunched up; there was safety in numbers. So, in effect, they searched only part of the hills.

Mark shook the leaves off when they passed and worked his way back toward the road. A piece of cake. He could hear no helicopters. Had the government suffered too many chopper crashes? They were damned expensive, after all. But in this kind of a search nothing would do the job as well. Whoever was in command had used poor judgement, he thought. Maybe the excitement of the chase . . .

He moved constantly westward, not wishing to come out onto the road near the parked trucks.

After a half hour had passed he heard a quick rattle of firearms from somewhere off to his right. The shots came and went over a period of five or six minutes.

Then silence.

Loughlin was somewhere in that direction.

When Mark finally poked his head out cautiously and looked up and down the road, there was no one and no vehicle in sight in either direction. He set out, walking on the shoulder, moving to the southwest at an easy pace. He ought to meet Hog any moment.

Hog Wiley went to the right, moving quickly. If he was fast enough, he'd outflank the men coming up from the road and be in the clear.

He knew soldiers—they would bitch and gripe about this kind of duty and probably make a half-assed job of it unless under the eye of an officer or stiff-necked N.C.O. And this search was a marvelous chance for goldbricking.

However, the pursuers were spread farther than he anticipated and he barely avoided them. A group of three came smashing through, one man in the lead with a machete, and passed by him almost close enough to touch. Hog lay in a tangle of weeds and grass, motionless as a stick, only his eyes moving.

When they had gone by, he got up and made his way back, following the path they had hacked. He found he was far along the road to the southwest, the trucks not in sight, so he made himself comfortable and waited.

Loughlin moved to the left, finding the going easier. He came across a game trail and followed it, bending half over, sometimes worming along on his belly but generally making good time. He heard the searchers come up the hill, but he easily avoided them; they were not spread far enough to the left.

But when he reached the road, he was seen.

One of the truck guards fired an AK at him as he jumped and rolled into a roadside ditch. He crawled away from the shooter at once, hearing shouts.

Out of sight of them he got to his feet and dived into a huge area of jungle grass, swearing a blue streak.

He heard men running, it sounded like two or three, and then shots were fired as they aimed at random into the growth where they thought he had gone. None of the shots came near.

He continued to crawl, unable to see his attackers, but he heard them exploring the area, hacking with machetes, firing now and then suspiciously.

When he was far enough away, he rose and quickly crossed the road. No shots came seeking him.

He was now on the north side of the parked trucks and would have to get by them to join up with Hog and Stone. It was in his favor that all the pursuers' attentions were directed to the other side of the road. But it was not to his advantage that there were large open areas in front of him. He would have to make his way around then, taking up time.

He swore mightily. It would take too goddamn much time. But he set out.

Hog Wiley rested for a bit, watching the road; no one appeared. Maybe Stone and Loughlin were far down the road waiting for him. Well, it wouldn't hurt to find out.

He was about to get to his feet when he heard engines. He ducked into the grass and in a few moments two BTR-60's came roaring past and disappeared in the distance.

He said aloud, "Hell of a lot of traffic for a dime's worth of road." He slung his weapons over his back and started out.

He met Stone in about fifteen minutes. Stone was sitting by the road, eyes half closed, taking it easy. He had not seen Loughlin, he said, but he'd heard the shots and wondered about them. "He could have met up with someone. What d'you think?"

"I think that Limey can take care of hisself. He's tough as Clancy's nuts. And damn near as smart."

Stone said, "Then let's move up to that hill. I like to be on high ground." He paused, turning his head.

Someone was firing a pistol. Maybe a recall.

The dirt road curved slightly, following the contours of the rounded hill, and they trudged up, keeping to the shoulder, ready to dash for cover in an instant. The countryside seemed very peaceful and calm. There were layers of high clouds overhead, thin as gossamer, and their boots crunched on the gravelly dirt. A few birds twittered and quarreled in the jungle just off the road, and Mark turned his head, hearing the sounds of a light-plane far in the distance.

They moved on quickly and came out on top of the hill into the open. A large area had been cleared of undergrowth and it looked as if an earthmover had been at work to level part of the ground.

Mark halted suddenly. Far to the right a Ford truck with canvas sides was parked.

Hog said, "What you figure—"

"Do not move, senores."

Looking over his shoulder, Mark saw a line of rifles pointing at them. He put his arms up.

Shit. A trap.

A slim young lieutenant moved around in front of them, a Walther pistol in his hand. "So—you are the *Americanos!* But we were told there were three of you. Where is the other one?"

"What other one?" Hog asked. "Never was but two of us. Somebody can't count."

The officer's eyes narrowed. "You are lying. You were counted a number of times."

Hog said amiably, "Folks never calls me a liar less'n they got a gun in their hands."

"We *know* there are three of you. Where is the other?"

Mark shrugged. "If there were three of us, he'd be here."

The lieutenant motioned with the pistol. "Take their weapons and tie them up."

Terrance Loughlin made a necessary wide swing to the north, skirting a huge open area where there was no cover unless he crawled, and he was tired of that. He rounded the fields and finally worked his way back to the road again, finding he was far to the southwest. The parked trucks were well behind him. When they were out of sight, he jogged along the deserted road, pausing now and then to listen.

The road curved and approached a rounded hill. He must be more than a mile from the trucks. He should have made contact with Hog and Stone long before this. They both should easily have avoided the troops sent to flush them out. He had heard several troop carriers go past on the road—had something happened?

But he'd heard no firing except a few stray pistol shots. If any group had gotten into a firefight with Hog and Stone, it certainly would have sounded like the battle of Gettysburg.

He had taken a lot more time than they to reach the road. Something must have happened. He looked at the sky, peered down the road, and suddenly felt very open and exposed. He moved into the tangle of jungle growth and rubbed his chin. It was damned curious.

Was it possible he had passed them? Could they both be back nearer the trucks? Not very bloody likely. He was sure the two would want to put distance between themselves and the soldiers.

He stepped out to the shoulder of the road, frowning at the hard-packed dirt, looking for telltale tracks, and seeing none. Scratching his chin, he looked up at the rounded hill where the road vanished. The two were probably up there waiting for him. But still, the silence was very suspicious.

Something *had* happened. He had a gut feeling that something was very wrong.

He crossed to the north side of the road and moved into the jungle, working his way up to the hill as silently as he could.

Maybe he was dead wrong and they'd smile at him for his caution. And maybe not.

It took forever. The growth was a thick tangle and even using his long-bladed knife he moved slowly. He'd have made short work of it all with a machete. . . .

When he knew by the feel of the ground that he had reached a position opposite the crown of the hill, he moved toward it, crawling the last hundred feet with extreme caution. He reached a place where he could see the cleared area atop the hill. There was a dark green canvas-draped truck standing there and a man inside with headphones, fiddling with a radio. Five or six men were sitting smoking in the shade of the truck.

Off to his right was a group of trees. Hog and Stone were standing there, hands tied behind their backs, facing two rifle-armed soldiers and an officer.

They had been captured.

Chapter Nine

The lieutenant's men disarmed Stone and Hog, frisking them thoroughly, taking every firearm, knife, and cartridge. Their wrists were tied together behind them with leather thongs and they were then roped to trees several feet apart.

The slim officer, whose name was Avila, holstered his pistol and smiled at them. "You are worth a good deal of money to me. I thank you for falling into my hands."

"How much *is* the reward?" Stone asked.

"Enough to make it important. But my superiors will want to know where your friend is."

"There was a young man with us a few days ago—"

"One of your countrymen?"

"No."

"Then he is not the one I seek. Where is your friend?"

Mark shook his head.

"Tell me, then, what is your business in Nicaragua?"

"We was thinking of raisin' goats," Hog said. "This looks like good goat country."

Avila's cheeks began to redden. His lips pressed together. "I must insist that you answer my questions. I am not a man to fool with."

"It looks like good weasel country, too," Hog continued. "I can see a lot of weasels right here."

The lieutenant moved suddenly and a leather quirt lashed out, snapping Hog's face around, leaving a white mark along one cheek that slowly turned red.

"Are you always this brave?" Stone asked. "Hitting men who are tied up?"

The officer's hand jerked and the quirt left a mark on Stone's cheek. Behind the lieutenant one of the soldiers snickered.

"Where is the other one?"

Stone shook his head again and the quirt lashed across his chest, tearing at his throat.

The officer screamed at him, "Where is the other one?" He lashed Hog. "Why are you in Nicaragua?"

Hog drawled, "We heard there was an asshole here that growed up to be a lootinant, and damn if that rumor wasn't right."

Avila shouted, assaulting them both with the quirt. Hog bowed his big shoulders and suffered the attack. Mark hauled on the ropes and blood streamed down their faces. The officer was a goddamned psycho!

But he tired in a few moments and stepped back, breathing hard, glaring at them. He snapped orders in Spanish, and the two men with rifles straightened. The lieutenant walked to the truck and climbed in. There was a tall aerial atop the cab. The man was doubtless reporting their capture.

Mark said, "You're ugly enough without getting yourself all cut to pieces."

"Can't help it," Hog replied. "A asshole is a asshole, no matter what uniform it wears."

"You're not put on earth to tell him so."

Hog sighed. "Guess I'm jus' impulsive."

"No speak," one of the guards said.

"Dumb is another word," Mark said. "His time will come."

Hog nodded. "Where the hell is that Limey?"

The guard growled. "No speak!"

Hog smiled at the man. "Go fuck yourself."

The man nodded.

An hour passed as slowly as ever it had in this world. The soldiers cooked food, no one gave them any, and after a bit the officer came out to smoke a cigarette and glare at them as if wondering what would make them talk. Mark could imagine that if Avila had reported their capture, his superiors had asked where the third man was — and Avila could not tell them. The reward might even be withheld, which would not increase Avila's consideration for them.

They saw him look at the glowing end of the cigarette, then he walked to them, smiling.

He halted in front of Stone. "Why are you in Nicaragua?"

"Everybody's got to be somewhere."

Avila had regained his composure. He smiled as the lion might, on meeting the lamb. "That is the wrong answer, my friend." He puffed on the cigarette. "I ask you once again. Why are you in Nicaragua?"

Hog said loudly, "Tell him the truth. We're here as part of the Anti-Asshole Society of the world."

Avila's face changed. He pressed the glowing end of the cigarette to Stone's cheek.

He smelled burning flesh. Mark jerked his head away and kicked out at Avila, but the slim man had been ready for it and easily sidestepped, laughing. Mark groaned, gritting his teeth. He heard Hog shout something, but the pain was a fire, consuming his head.

In that moment, while everyone was looking at Mark, Loughlin jumped into the open with a great yell.

The Uzi in his hands spat fire, cutting down the two guards behind Avila. He rushed at the lieutenant, who tugged at his pistol and slumped with three shots in his chest, his face white, eyes staring.

The Uzi scattered the men at the truck, toppling four like ninepins. The radioman scrambled to get into the truck and slid down, crumpled in the dirt. Three men dived into the jungle, screaming in terror, smashing their way . . . and the Uzi clicked empty.

Loughlin yanked out the magazine and replaced it, running toward the jungle. He fired several bursts in the direction of the sounds, then ran back to Hog and Mark and quickly sliced the ropes that bound them to the trees.

"Where the hell you been?" Hog said. "You missed all the goddamn fun!"

"I had a date at the club. Couldn't get away. Sorry." He gave the knife to Hog and jogged to the truck.

One of the soldiers rolled onto his belly and snapped a shot at Loughlin, who blasted him and the other three. He went close, kicking them to make sure. The radioman had a slug through his forehead.

When he went back to the others, Avila was still alive, gasping and coughing, his eyes wide and scared. He tried to talk, but Loughlin nudged him with the Uzi. "Shut up, asshole."

Hog said, "Ask him what he's doin' in Nicaragua."

It had all happened seemingly in the wink of an eye. Nothing like surprise. Loughlin had picked exactly the right moment to come charging in, screaming like a mad thing, firing the submachine gun with deadly accuracy. The soldiers had had no time to think and could only react by running. Three men had gotten away.

Hog brought Mark the first aid kit from the truck's glove compartment. There was a tube of salve for burns. He smeared his cheek with it and the pain began to recede.

Hog stood over Avila. The man was dying. He took the officer's pistol, and Avila's lips moved. He wanted to say something, but Hog walked away, looking the pistol over. It had not been fired. He put it in his belt.

They investigated the Ford truck. It was in fair condition. The gas tank was more than half full and there was a spare can in the back holding two gallons. There was a cardboard box of rations, some ammo, and a stack of dark blue blankets. The radio was in working order, and Loughlin quickly tuned to a station with music.

When Mark went back to look at Avila, the man was dead. Tough shit. They dragged the other bodies into the jungle and got out, with Hog driving the truck. All in all, it had been a busy day.

It was close to evening when they came to the railroad tracks. Hog pulled up and they consulted the map, deciding they must be about *here*. Loughlin drew a circle with a pencil. A road of sorts paralleled the tracks.

"What you think . . . the railroad probably goes to Managua, huh?"

"Sounds logical," Mark agreed. "Let's try it."

Hog fired up the engine and they crossed the tracks and turned left. It was an even worse road than the one they had just followed. The railroad curved through the hills, the road crossed it, then crossed back, and after a half hour Hog said, "Village up ahead. The road goes smack through it, amigos. You want we should stop and have a look or go on through?"

"It's getting dark," Mark said. "We could go through, waving like tourists. . . ."

"That gets my vote," Loughlin said. "But lemme get in the back in case there's a welcoming committee." He slipped out the door and climbed into the back end. Mark checked his Uzi.

As they came close they could see a jeep and a small Japanese-made pickup truck in the street. Two soldiers were sitting in the jeep. Hog never slowed but drove through at a steady pace as Mark waved from the side window. A few people stared at them and a man ran into the road, shouting something. They ignored him.

It took only a few moments to leave the village behind, then they were in open country again. Stone fiddled with the radio, but all they got was music or too-rapid Spanish, so he settled for the music. Loughlin climbed back into the cab to say he was getting hungry.

"Hell," Hog said, slapping the wheel, "we're in tall corn. Iffen we had some gals, we could have us a party."

"If we had some wings and tailfeathers, we could be in Managua in an hour," Mark said, feeling his cheek.

"If we had some—" Loughlin began.

"Enough," Mark said wearily. "Let's look for a spot t'stop."

"Why don't we keep agoin'?"

"Because we could run into God knows what. Those guys at that last village probably phoned ahead."

Loughlin shrugged. "How could they know it was us?"

"They don't, but we didn't stop. That in itself is suspicious to the locals. Maybe they have a rule or something—or a password."

Hog said glumly, "We shoulda squeezed it outa the asshole—whatever his name was." He glanced at Loughlin. "Damn you, I was figgerin' to get my hands on him."

Mark laughed. "Yeah, Terrance, I would have loved to see that, too. You're a spoilsport."

Loughlin sighed deeply. "I should know better than to rescue you guys. Especially when you're having all that fun."

Hog said, slowing down, "I think that's a spot up ahead. Let's check it out." He turned off the road and stopped the truck in a grove of trees.

Mark said, "I'll take a look." He walked back toward the road and turned. It was remarkable how the green canvas sides of the truck blended in. The bulky thing could not be seen at all in the darkness.

He cocked his head, hearing engines, and got down to lie flat. The jeep and the Japanese-made pickup passed by on the road, and he thought they were loaded with men. It was hard to tell in the gloom. It was impossible to know if they were headed that way anyhow, or were chasing *Norte Americanos*. He got up, watching the headlights fade away in the distance, then shrugged and went back to the truck. They might have to leave the vehicle and walk the rest of the way. . . .

Managua could not be far now.

His thoughts wandered to the two C.I.A. men held by the Sandinistas. The chances were they were not being harmed; but they were probably undergoing intensive interrogation. And that might be extremely uncomfortable.

He shook his head. How in the world would they get to General Romero Perez? It could easily prove the most difficult feat in Nicaragua. For *Norte Americanos*. Well, best not to worry about it now. There were immediate things—save that worry for later.

First they had to get into the capital. *That* alone was proving hard enough. Every soul in the country seemed to know about them, and since there was a reward—so the Asshole had told them—people would shoot to kill on sight. He could think of more pleasant things.

Paco hurried his two carriers to the road and set up an ambush—but the fugitives did not appear. He had guessed wrong again. They must have taken another road—unless they had gone over the hills on foot. What a task he had been given—to find three wily men in hundreds of square miles!

His radio was now "repaired," and Major Rosas had calmed down. Paco did his best diplomatically to explain that, with the few men he had at his disposal, it was impossible to cover all the roads and trails.

Rosas countered that no more men were available. There was a civil war to fight, after all, and *his* superiors were beginning to ask pointed questions. Rosas strongly suggested that Paco show some results, or he would be replaced.

When the one-sided conversation was over, Paco shouted at the passing scenery that he was not God! He did not have the ability to see through walls or into men's minds! How could any sensible person think like a fucking *Norte Americano* anyhow? If he was so smart, let Major Rosas come into the field and show his brilliance!

But of course it did little good.

Sergeant Cortes brought him a report about a squad of men who had mysteriously disappeared, along with a Lieutenant Avila and a troop-carrying truck. "They are long overdue," Cortes said. "Maybe they met the men we are after and the truck was stolen from them."

It was possible. Grumpily Paco agreed to backtrack and investigate the occurrence. By radio he learned the officer and men had been ordered to a particular location and had not appeared. A cursory search had not turned them up.

Paco turned his carriers around and went back—and found nothing.

But they picked up a message, as they were searching, that three men of that squad had turned up in another sector with a story of having been nearly killed by a crazy man with a machine gun. They'd had very little time to observe, but all three had the same impression —the man had been a *Norte Americano*.

Paco went at once to interrogate them.

He found them in a small village under guard. A company of men under a stout captain was in charge and very suspicious of the story. He was sure, he told Paco, that the men were merely deserters.

Paco had them brought out and placed in a small room. They were calm now and could tell their story coherently. They had been part of a ten-man squad, under a Lieutenant Avila whom they did not know. They were being sent somewhere; they only shrugged when

Paco asked where. Avila had appeared and counted them off and ordered them into the truck.

At any rate, they had captured two *Norte Americanos*—

"Two?" Paco asked.

"Two, sir." Avila had said they were worth a great deal of reward money and they would all share in it. Avila had ordered the two men tied up and roped to trees. Then the lieutenant had tortured them.

"Tortured?" Paco said in surprise.

The three men nodded vigorously. Avila had been aggressive in trying to get information from the captives . . . who had insulted the officer even though tied up.

"What did he do?"

"He beat them and burned them with a cigarette, sir."

"And what did the prisoners tell him?"

The men shook their heads. "Nothing, sir. But they had no time. The madman appeared."

"Tell me," Paco said.

"A wild man ran from the jungle, yelling at the top of his voice—with a machine gun!"

"Ahhh," Paco said, "the third *Norte Americano!* Do you tell me he killed seven men?"

"Oh, yes, sir. And would have killed us, too—"

"But you are brave *soldados*, you ran into the jungle. You dropped your weapons and ran . . . is that not so?"

They hung their heads.

"You were ten to one and you ran?"

"He took us by surprise, sir!"

Paco's lip curled. "You are scum. Get out of my sight!" He ordered them handcuffed and thrown into one of the carriers. "No one is to talk to them. No one!"

With their directions, Paco drove at once to the rounded hill. They quickly discovered the bodies of the soldiers and the lieutenant. Paco radioed for someone to come and carry them away.

Then he sent out word for all units to be on the look-out for a Ford truck with green canvas sides.

They tossed a coin and decided to go on with the truck. With Loughlin at the wheel they set out at midnight and drove until nearly dawn, passing three villages and a number of parked vehicles. Only once were they hailed, and they ignored it. A burst of AK fire followed them. It ripped and shredded the canvas on one side of the truck.

Morning found them parked in a forest well off the road, in a hilly section. With daylight; they made a small fire in a draw and heated coffee. Their rations were getting low, even with what they had found in the truck. They would have to liberate some soon, Mark said, or go hungry.

"Hongry is not my thing," Hog said definitely. "How you say beans in Spanish, frijoles?"

"Frijoles."

"All right, next village we come to I'll go in and yell frijoles. See what we can scare up. But I wisht we had us some good ol' Texas chili."

"And fish'n chips to go with it," Loughlin said wist-fully.

Mark said, "As long as you're wishing, let's wish for something sensible."

"That's right." Hog nodded. "We oughta wish fer some gals."

When they started out again, they ran into a road-block in the first five miles.

There were two Russki trucks and a jeep parked squarely across the narrow road.

Stone was driving and he could see instantly there was no way around. He jammed on the brakes, backed up, and turned around—as shots were fired at them and men scurried.

"Get in the back!" Mark yelled. "Keep them off our tail!"

He pushed the gas pedal to the floor. The road was very rutted. It had not been scraped since Balboa had discovered the Pacific, and the big truck bounced and swayed. Not a good platform for shooting.

Hog and Loughlin quickly climbed through the door and into the truck bed and in a moment were firing back.

Mark could see, in the side-view mirror, that the trucks and the jeep were following, at a respectful distance. The AK bursts from the back of the Ford were telling.

"Aim at the tires!" Hog yelled.

They got the jeep first. It swerved off the road with a shredded front tire, and the trucks dropped back farther.

Stone decided to take the first promising road that led toward the left . . . west. The two in the back were firing short bursts now and then. The assault rifles had a long range. After ten or fifteen minutes they set up a cheering. Mark peered at the mirror. One of the big trucks had slewed around and was stopping, blocking the other. They must have hit the driver.

They lost sight of the pursuers for the next few miles, but the road he hoped for did not show up. When they came to the first village, men were hurriedly piling up boxes and debris to form a roadblock; the radio had alerted them. But they were not in time. Mark gunned the Ford through, smashing the boxes and sending the other boards flying. Hog fired from one side and Loughlin the other, and they were past, into the open again.

But they were going the wrong goddamn way!

When they finally came to a crossroads, Mark slowed and turned left, crossing the railroad tracks, moving into the hills. How long would it take for the helicopters or planes to find them? He yelled for one of them to come up and study the map, and in a few moments Loughlin climbed into the cab again.

"We smashed the truck up proper, chum. They may

have to junk it unless they have a hell of a lot of Russki parts."

"Nice going," Mark said. "Get the map out."

Loughlin spread it on his knees, finding the penciled circle he'd made before. He clucked and frowned over the map, moving his finger . . . and decided. "Here. We must be just about here." He took out the pencil and made another circle. "We're not gaining much, you know, going backwards."

"I don't understand why—we're doing a hell of a lot of driving."

"It's probably that kilometers are shorter than miles."

Mark sighed deeply, watching the rearview mirror. The pursuit was not visible; no one behind them at the moment. Had they gotten away? Probably not.

Loughlin folded up the map and pointed to the gas gauge. "Getting low on petrol, chum. Better stop at the next station. Get the windscreen cleaned, too."

Mark grunted and swung around a sharp turn—and braked hard.

In front of them was a formidable roadblock.

And a dozen or more rifles pointing at them.

There was no room to do anything, not even back up. Men swarmed behind them and a burst of fire screamed over their heads. Hog was swearing.

They were prisoners.

Chapter Ten

Stone saw instantly that their captors were not Sandinistas. They were Contra rebels. Men pushed close to the truck, then made way for an officer with a braided cap. He said curiously to Stone, "You are the *Norte Americanos*."

Mark nodded. "You heard about us on the radio?"

"Sí, senor. You are famous! Come, you are our guests!"

They got out of the truck and the officer introduced himself. "I am Captain Jose Ortega. In the States you call us freedom-fighters, do you not?"

"Yes, I think so . . ." Mark smiled. "Did you get your money from congress?"

Ortega shrugged. "I have seen no money."

It did not look as if they had. All of the men were poorly dressed in cotton shirts and pants. Their weapons were mostly those liberated from the government troops, but their spirit seemed high.

Ortega took them around the hill by a narrow, covered path; covered, he said, against nosy aircraft and their bombs.

There were well-camouflaged huts and caves. He

took them into one of the huts where there were chairs and a bench and a wide table. This was where they held meetings, Ortega told them. He had studied in the States, in California, in fact. "I want to be a veterinarian when this is all over." He had come home to fight for his country against Communist invaders. "When we win, I will go back and finish my studies."

"I hope it's soon," Mark said.

A woman brought them food, and as they ate, Ortega said they had been monitoring the Sandinista radio and knew quite a bit about the notorious *Norte Americanos*. "There is a large reward for your death or captures, senores. Somehow you have made them very angry. It is a great shame."

"They kind of riled us up, too," Hog told him, attacking a plate of beans. "We shore didn't get along from the start."

"They wonder what you are doing in Nicaragua."

"They mentioned that . . ." Loughlin made a face.

"We fight for freedom, too," Mark said seriously, "in our own way. It is true we have a mission that we hope will hurt them very much. Can you help us get to Managua?"

Ortega studied them. "Yes, I can give you a guide, but not much else. I have only thirty men and no money. We are a thorn in their sides. . . ." He shrugged again. "I am sorry to say you cannot go farther in your truck. Every government soldier in the area is looking for it. You would be bombed from the air."

Loughlin asked, "Can we trade it to you for another car?"

"We do not have a car, senores." He poured some wine for them and sat down, lighting a fat cigar. He smiled. "My best offer is the guide."

Mark asked, "Do you really have hopes of winning? You've been fighting them for five years, after all."

"We can win if we get enough aid from Washington —from your congress. We need many things."

"Your enemies say you have made no significant gains in all the years you've opposed the government and that your army has no real bases in Nicaragua."

Ortega puffed smoke. "I am the leader of a very small group, senores. I do not know anything about high strategy. My men and I do what we can. We are gaining recruits slowly, and I am told we are gaining footholds. Our enemies are trained by Cubans and by the Communists of Russia, and they are ruthless. But we will fight them to the death."

An airplane droned overhead, and Ortega glanced up at the ceiling of the hut. "We need aircraft...." He shrugged, looking at the cigar ash. "When I went to school in your country, I read about your revolution from Britain, and about Valley Forge. Sometimes I think we are now in our own Valley Forge, or something maybe even worse. Because if we lose, we will have the evil of Communism on the mainland of America."

"That damn well ain't good," Hog commented.

The understatement of the year, Mark thought.

Another aircraft buzzed overhead, high up, and in moments a helicopter gunship skirted the hills, moving along parallel to the railroad tracks.

"They are looking for the Ford truck," Ortega said, standing in the doorway of the hut. "They will not find it."

"Have you hidden it?"

"*Sí.* My people have taken it into a cave. We will take it apart and change it altogether. It is our first truck, and I thank you for it." He smiled at them. "Will you have more wine?"

Hog accepted, emptying the flask.

Ortega left them for a bit and returned with a young man he introduced as Fortun Deppe, once a farmer's son. Fortun was lithe and brown with very white teeth. He was dressed like the others in cotton shirt and pants, with a Smith & Wesson revolver strapped about his narrow hips. He spoke better English than most, Ortega said, and he knew every inch of the ground between here and Managua. "You can trust him completely."

Fortun grinned at them, saying he was pleased to meet them, then he hurried out to get his kit together. Ortega said, when the lad had gone, "His mother is alive in Honduras, but the Sandinistas killed his father and brother while they were working in the fields unarmed, provoking no one. Fortun has avenged them several times." Ortega shook his head sadly. "There is much hate in Nicaragua."

They set out in an hour, walking south with Fortun in the lead, a captured AK assault rifle slung over his shoulder with a cartridge belt. They marched in single file with Loughlin bringing up the rear. They wound over the hills under a wide blue sky, with the sounds of gunships coming closer. The choppers were making circles, as Ortega had said, looking for the Ford truck they would never find.

Fortun seemed to know exactly how close a chopper could come to them before they were seen. When he signaled, they all flattened themselves until it veered away.

They saw five lightplanes and choppers that afternoon. A vigorous pursuit must be on, Mark Stone thought. What would happen to them if they were caught? An execution? Probably a prolonged interrogation of each man first— then execution. Thinking of interrogation, he touched his cheek. It was very sore and he kept it well covered with the salve, but it never allowed him to forget it.

As the long shadows lengthened, the search came their way. Fortun then led them into a deep ravine, and they trudged along it for a mile or more until they came to an overhanging cliff; then they sat in deep shade as the aircraft passed overhead with rotors beating their monotonous song. They were not spotted and the choppers drifted away.

Fortun seemed to have no great fear of them; they

were deadly in some circumstances, but when a man had a ditch to protect him and a good automatic weapon, the chopper had better sheer off. He had shot down one, he told them, and would do it again if he found one alone.

The helicopters were called off toward evening; they all whirled away to the east and the rotor song faded. Fortun suggested they travel a bit farther before dark; he had a destination in mind. Not far away was a region of more rugged hills where their cover would be better, and Mark agreed.

When they halted at last it was a deep valley, heavily wooded, by a muddy pond. Well hidden by the canopy of trees were several uninhabited shacks used by travelers, Fortun said. He assured them that a fire would not be seen by an enemy. "The Sandinistas do not come into these hills unless in great force."

Mark asked, "Do you know the city?"

"A little. I have spent no time there."

"Do you know of any rebel groups in the city?"

"No, but I know someone who would know." Fortun indicated their clothes. "You cannot go into the city in daylight dressed like this."

Loughlin nodded. "We'll have to liberate some Sandinista uniforms, just in case."

They were up early in the morning and under way, threading a path through the hills with the choppers far off to the left, still quartering the ground. Whoever was in command was persistent. Fortun avoided all villages and farmhouses. They could see field workers in the distance now and again, and once they lay in tall grass while a Sandinista patrol, twenty or thirty strong, passed with equipment jangling.

"We will meet more of them," Fortun said softly. "I regret we cannot set an ambush for them. But Captain Ortega—" He shrugged.

Obviously Ortega had given him explicit instructions.

The region was more settled and they had to detour many times to avoid meeting field workers or travelers, and occasionally soldiers. Fortun advised even avoiding rebel forces, saying that all their leaders were not as sophisticated as Captain Ortega and might detain them.

They assumed he meant that some were less likely to smile on wandering *Norte Americanos* who were armed to the teeth and apparently had no business in their country.

They skirted a large plain, traversed a series of low hills, and crossed a fast-running stream, all very peaceful and quiet. Nicaragua was a beautiful country, Stone thought. Too bad it was caught up in a terrible civil war.

In late afternoon they came to the edge of a stand of oaks and saw in the distance what seemed to be a tower and an airfield. Fortun confirmed that it was indeed a small military field, an airstrip and a helicopter pad owned by the government. "We have noted there are troops stationed there, sometimes as many as a hundred."

Hog rubbed his chin. "Maybe we can steal us a plane?" He glanced around. "Anyone fly one of them things?"

No one could. Fortun had never been up in one, he said. He did not sound eager to do so.

"Well," Loughlin remarked to the air. "If we can't steal a plane, maybe we can smash one or two. I'm goddamn tired of twisting my neck watching out for them."

"Me too," Hog agreed. "Them buggers is askin' for it."

Stone looked at Fortun. "Is it possible to get onto the field?"

"Oh, yes. But Captain Ortega has given me—"

"The captain ain't here," Hog said, glancing around as if he expected to see him. "And what he don't know ain't gonna bite his ass. You don't want to burn up a airplane? What kind of a rebel are you, anyways?"

"Oh, I want to," Fortun assured him as the others laughed.

The airfield, when they came nearer, sat in the shadow of a line of hills on a level bit of ground that had probably been bulldozed. The strip itself was paved and blacktopped and was very narrow. The tower was some forty feet above the ground and had what seemed to be a single room with a drooping flag on top. Even with the binoculars they could see no one in it.

There was a low hangar and three other buildings. Three lightplanes were parked by the hangar beside a small truck where two men fussed.

As they crawled along a deep furrow and reached a position near the west fence, chain link, in a drainage ditch, a chopper came in to land. It settled down on the pad and the rotors ground to a halt as two men got out and walked to one of the buildings.

"Three planes and a chopper," Stone said, rubbing his hands together. "That'll cost 'em."

Hog asked. "How much one of them whirlybirds worth?"

"Plenty," Loughlin said. "More'n the planes."

"I don't see any soldiers," Stone remarked.

"They drive around the fence," Fortun said. "Maybe they wait until dark."

"We will, too," Stone said, nodding. "The fence looks easy to climb. In the meantime, let's take it easy."

Two more lightplanes landed before dark and were lined up neatly with the others. At dusk a string of lights came on, illuminating the aircraft, creating deep shadows. There was no activity on the field at all. A half dozen soldiers or workmen hung about the hangar door talking and smoking, but at full dark they too disappeared, and the big hangar door was pushed closed.

Three men opened a door in one of the other buildings and drove a jeep out and fiddled with it a bit. Hog thought they were loading a machine gun on the car. It was difficult to see, even with the binoculars.

Finally they got in and drove off to the north fence.

"They think they are safe here," Fortun said, smiling. "We have not attacked this airstrip before."

"Now's the day," Hog observed. "Got to be a first time for ever'thing."

Loughlin asked, "What's the plan, chums? How's the best way t'do this?"

Fortun surprised them. "Do you have grenades? I have only four."

Stone laughed. "We have a few." They each had two in their packs, with the handles taped down. They were standard U.S. issue M-26's with eight-second fuses, fragmentation type.

"We open the plane door, drop them inside—one ought to do for each plane—then run like hell. Fortun and I'll do the planes. We'll leapfrog. I'll do one and three, Fortun'll do two and four. And one of us will get the fifth while the other gets the chopper. All right?"

Fortun nodded.

"What about them lights?" Hog asked, scratching his chin. "Soon's we put 'em out, the guys on the jeep will come tearin' in to ask questions."

"Terry will get the lights and you take out the jeep," Stone told him. "The jeep and anyone else who shows his nose. Can do?"

"Piece of cake," Hog said, fondling the Uzi. He peered at the darkened field. "Where's the barracks, shorty? Where do the soldiers hang out?"

Fortun said, "There's a barracks building behind the hangar. If they hear shooting, they will come around the end of the hangar."

"Unless they don't."

"*Sí*, unless they come some other way. But that is the quickest."

Hog grinned. "I'll keep my eye on it."

"All right," Stone told them. "Surprise in everything. We run across the field to the last building on the right. That's the first stop. From there we douse the lights. There may be a box on one of the walls. If not, Terrance will shoot them out."

"Right-o, mate."

"Then Fortun and I will dump grenades in the planes and chopper. Hog and Terrance will cover us." He looked at them. "Questions?"

"Then we all chase off the field—where?"

"It depends on where the jeep is. If we can keep the buildings between us and it."

"OK."

"Gotcha," Hog said.

Chapter Eleven

It took only moments to climb the fence. The jeep was on the far side of the field behind the buildings. With Fortun in the lead, they jogged across the dark field to the shelter of the last building. It was a good fifty yards from the string of lights, and they stood in deep shadow, listening.

They could hear only the engine of the jeep as it made its monotonous rounds. Now and then one of the three in the car switched on a floodlight to illuminate something or other—maybe only from boredom.

They let it make a round and go behind the buildings again. Then Mark touched Loughlin. "Do it."

Loughlin stepped out casually, walked along the building to the next, his eyes on the wires. He stopped, and they saw him flick out his long knife. He glanced toward them and his arms jerked—and the lights went out.

Stone and Fortun raced to the planes. Mark ran to the last plane and yanked at the door. It seemed to be fastened. He smashed the glass with the butt of his Uzi, tossed the grenade in, and ran to the third plane. Fortun waited till he passed, then tossed his bomb inside. He followed Mark, waited till Mark dropped the second grenade, then he tossed the fourth.

The first grenade exploded, shattering the silence of the field. As Mark dropped the fifth grenade an alarm bell began to ring in one of the buildings. The second grenade exploded with a roar. The first plane was burning briskly—the third grenade exploded.

Fortun tossed a grenade into the helicopter and ran into the dark field with Mark and Loughlin close behind. With his Uzi at the ready, Hog backed toward them, watching for the jeep...as the fourth grenade went up, tossing the lightplane like a rag doll. In a moment the jeep came into view, its floodlight on, and the grenade in the chopper went off with a smashing roar.

Hog's Uzi stuttered and the jeep slewed at once, and the floodlight was doused.

Fortun yelled, "Run—run!" He made for the fence.

Men spilled from one of the buildings, and Loughlin went to one knee, firing a long burst as Hog dashed past him. A few shots came toward them as men fired wildly. Mark returned the fire as Fortun went over the fence. The men on the field scattered. No one fired at them as they climbed the fence and jumped into the drainage ditch. The planes were burning fiercely—no one would put them out. Fortun yelled at them to follow, climbed out of the ditch, and ran directly away from the field.

Mark glanced back as they ran into the darkness. It was a marvelous success, and surprise had been the most important element. Surprise was worth a hundred men.

In two hours they were deep in the hills. Fortun halted them in a cavelike area with sheltering trees, saying this was a refuge often used. The raid had gone like clockwork, all aircraft destroyed. The enemy would be raging.

"It woulda cost them less iffen they'd give us a pass across Nicaragua," Hog said, grinning.

* * *

Lieutenant Paco Suran was furious. The Ford truck with the green canvas sides could not be found. It was either hidden somewhere or it had been so changed it was unrecognizable. But every vehicle on the roads, especially those heading for Managua, was being stopped and searched.

The *Norte Americanos* were not to be found either. And he, Paco, was in trouble. The messages from Major Rosas were getting more and more biting. As a result, Paco's radio continually needed "repairs."

When the report came to him concerning the raid on the airfield, Paco headed there immediately. The commandant was a retired colonel, impressed into service, named Bandini. They met in Bandini's spartan office. The older man was lined and gray. He had lost six aircraft, he said, including a helicopter, and felt himself lucky that the entire group of buildings had not been fired.

"What did your men see, sir?"

"A group of raiders. Two of my men counted ten, all armed with submachine guns. They came from two directions, killed two men driving the jeep and wounded the third. Killed one man at the door of the building and wounded four. They were devils!"

Paco had heard that term before. He said, "Ten raiders? Are you positive, sir?"

The old man drew himself up. "My men do not lie, sir."

"Of course not. I only thought—in the heat of battle —a man could be mistaken."

The colonel stared at him. "Why do you doubt it?"

"I am hunting three men, sir. And—"

"Three!? Impossible! Three men could not have caused the damage!"

Paco nodded. "It does not seem possible."

"There are many rebels in the hills, Lieutenant. This raid was the work of one of them, I am positive. They

come like shadows and they leave like shadows after
their terrible work is finished. It is apparent this raid
was planned for a long time. They struck at an opportune moment when we were very short-handed. You
will have to look elsewhere for your three men."

Paco was nearly convinced. He talked to several of
the men of the base, but their colonel had declared the
raid to be the work of at least ten men and no one con-
tradicted him.

It was very frustrating. If there *had* been ten men
involved, then Paco was sure the *Norte Americanos* had
joined up with a rebel group. He could *smell* their presence.

But when he talked to Major Rosas on the radio, he
told Rosas the airfield raid was definitely not the work
of the men they sought. The three *Norte Americanos*
were obviously hiding somewhere underground like
rabbits, afraid to show their noses.

It mollified Rosas to some extent. For once he did
not mention tacking Paco's skin to the wall.

Fortun was delighted with the success of the raid.
He confessed that it had gone better than he had expected, and he was most impressed with the accuracy of
their shooting.

But the enemy would increase his efforts. They must
now travel at night to escape detection. "It will be
slower," Fortun said, "but it will be safer. And we will
not have to worry about helicopters."

They moved a few miles early in the morning; then,
when the aircraft began droning overhead, they laid up,
resting, using the time to clean weapons.

At dusk Fortun led out again, insisting they travel in
single file, in silence. They were getting close to habita-
tions, he told them, the city was not far. They crossed
railroad tracks, approaching a siding where cars stood
near brown buildings that might have been a machine

shop. There was traffic on a highway nearby, but they got across it without being seen and into low hills. The lad led them around a sprawling village and across fields into a wooded area where a stream wandered.

Just before dawn they found a wide ravine and Fortun said. "I have brought you almost as far as I can. The city is very near."

Mark said, "I've been thinking about that. We are to contact a man named Jorge Mora at a café, the Copa de Leche. He has information we need."

Loughlin spoke up. "You said you had a friend who knows the city and other rebels."

"*Sí*. I will go into the city and find him."

Hog said, "*He* could go to the café for us. Fortun."

Mark nodded, studying Fortun. "That might be the best way all around. The fewer who know about us the better. What do you say, shortstop?"

Fortun grinned. "Maybe so. What part of the city is the café in?"

"We don't know."

"No matter. I will ask. And when I find this Jorge Mora, what do I say to him?"

"You bring him to us. The password is Colonel Bill Haskins."

"Colonel Haskins? That is a password?"

Mark nodded. "It will identify you. Mora is expecting someone."

Fortun looked at the sky. "Then I will go into the city at midday. I should be back by night."

They settled down to wait. They were on high ground, and when the sun came up they could see the city in the near distance. Smoke was rising from hundreds of chimneys and stacks and far off to the left they could see part of the lake shimmering in the early sun. Below them on the hills were homes and from somewhere a bell was tolling.

Fortun unbuckled his revolver and tucked it into his

waistband at his back, with the shirt hanging free over it. He would not go without it.

When he was ready to go, Mark said, *"Que le vaya bien."*

Fortun grinned. "Don't take any wooden—what is it you say?"

"Nickels."

"Sí. Nickels." He waved and was gone, climbing out of the ravine and hurrying across the field to a row of trees. He waved once more and disappeared.

The day passed on leaden hours for Stone and his men. They kept a watch and slept, but no one came near. Aircraft landed somewhere near in the haze and now and then they could hear city noises, but very far off. Hog said a dozen times, "I wish to hell I'd gone with him."

"You would be in jail by now, *Americano,"* Loughlin said, with a thick Spanish accent.

Fortun looked exactly like a thousand others. No one paid him the slightest attention. He asked directions to the Copa de Leche and went there at once. It was in a poor section of the city on a street that was brave with new paint; it was all facade. Fortun walked past, then went around the block and made his way to the back of the café, where several cars were parked.

A heavy-set man was arguing with the driver of a truck. As Fortun came near the driver yelled something, put the truck in gear, and roared away as the heavy-set man glared after him and shook his head. The man then scowled at Fortun. "What d'you want here? Go and scavenge somewhere else!"

"I am not a beggar," Fortun said.

The man grunted, turned on his heel, and walked to the back door of the café.

Fortun said, "Wait!" The man halted and Fortun hurried to him. "Do you work here, senor?"

"I am part owner. What do you want?"

"I'm looking for Jorge Mora. Do you know him?"

The man frowned. "I do not know him. Why do you come here for him? He is a very bad man and I want nothing to do with him! If you are his friend—go away and do not come back!"

"But, I am told he is often here!"

"That is not true!" The man's face was showing anger. "I do not allow him to come here!"

Fortun was surprised but suddenly recalled the password. "Colonel Haskins," he said.

The man's face changed in an instant. He grabbed Fortun's arm and walked with him away from the door. He glanced over his shoulder. "That is different." He shrugged. "One must be very careful of the police, you understand. They are everywhere!"

"Then you know Mora?"

"Of course I know him. But there is a price on his head. The police and the army want him badly—they will shoot him on sight. Where do you come from?"

"I belong to Captain Ortega's group—you do not know them."

"Why do you want Mora?"

"I am only the go-between. I have friends who must meet with him." Did he dare say they were *Norte Americanos?*

The heavy-set man's grip tightened on his arm. His voice was suddenly soft as he pulled Fortun closer. "And who are these friends, amigo?"

"Can I trust you?"

"It is good to be cautious. Colonel Haskins is a *Norte Americano* who is a friend of the people, not the government. I am expecting to hear from him. Tell me, who are the friends?"

"I do not know if I am allowed to say."

The big man regarded him steadily, then glanced about the alley. "We cannot stand here all day. You must tell me."

Fortun sighed. "What is your name?"

"I am Roberto." He moved his head. "I can be found any day at this café."

Fortun made up his mind. "They are *Norte Americanos.*" He saw the other relax. It was the right answer.

"Bueno. I have been waiting for this message. Where are your friends?"

"They are hidden on the outskirts of the city."

"Ahhh. Do you know this section?"

Fortun shook his head.

"Then I will send someone with you. You will need a guide. She knows where Mora is hiding."

"A woman?"

Roberto looked at him coldly. "Do you have something against women? I assure you, she hates Sandinistas as much as you."

"No, no, no, I was only surprised."

"Very well." Roberto released him. "Wait here. I will send Eva out to you."

"Eva?"

"Sí. Her name is Eva Castelo." Roberto strode to the door of the café.

Chapter Twelve

Eva Castelo was a young, lithe, and beautiful girl, though she was dressed in shapeless clothes, her black hair drawn back severely, tied with a black ribbon.

She asked him, "What is the name you told Roberto?"

"Colonel Bill Haskins."

She smiled. *"Si.* Then we will go."

She took him to a car, a very old VW beetle painted dark red with black designs by some fanciful artist with a penchant for dragons. She slid behind the wheel, and as she settled herself, Fortun saw that she was armed with a pistol.

He said, "You do not live in the city?"

"I live in the mountains—as you do."

"What if we are stopped by the police?" He shrugged. "I have no papers."

Her hand moved under her clothes and came out with a pistol with a long barrel. "Then we will use this."

Fortun grinned. The pistol had a silencer.

She said, "You are no good to us in jail."

"Very true."

Eva drove with caution, constantly on the lookout for

police, not wishing to draw attention to them. When she left the main street, they were in a section of poor red-tile roofed houses and rutted dirt streets with no curbs. She made many turns, her eyes on the rearview mirror. "No one is following us."

They passed into a district that was fast going to seed. It had been industrial, but the buildings were rusting, falling into decay, fences down, windows without glass and roofs disintegrating. No one lived in the district. She turned into a street that was little more than a wide gutter, and then into an alley. It was a tunnel-like affair but cleared of debris, and the little car ran to the end of it, stopping before a pair of garagelike doors that barred the way.

"Open the doors," she told him.

Fortun got out. The doors were secured by a large wooden pin. He drew it out, it hung by a rope, and pushed the doors open. He was surprised that they opened at once—the hinges were well oiled. Eva drove though and killed the engine. "Close them quickly."

Fortun closed the doors and looked around. He was in a huge, cavernous room, littered with every kind of junk. The roof was open to the skies in many places and the walls at the far end were tumbling down. There was a dusty board floor and the place had the look of an ex-factory.

Eva left the little car and walked to the end wall to the right of the double doors. Glancing around, she took up a stick and banged on a vertical pipe, three, then one, then two.

Someone answered from above with the same raps.

She said, "Come up, muchacho." She opened a door that he had not noticed, and he saw steps. They went up dark, creaking stairs and a door above them opened. A man stood there with a submachine gun pointed in their direction.

He smiled, seeing Eva. "Ahhh, the most beautiful

girl in all Nicaragua." He stared at Fortun. "And who is this one?"

"My name is Fortun. I am from the country."

"You are with Eva . . ." The man beckoned. "Come in, close the door."

"He is a guide," Eva said. "He has friends outside the city. They would come here."

Fortun said, "The password is Colonel Haskins."

"Ahhh, that makes a difference!" The man took Fortun's hand and shook it. "Welcome, welcome. I am Jorge Mora. What is it your friends want? I was told they would come here."

"I do not know, sir." Fortun looked about him. He was in a small room, furnished with only a cot bed and two rickety-looking chairs, a bench, and a table. There was a small portable stove on the table, some clothes draped over the chairs, and a Colt .45 automatic on the cot. There was another in Mora's belt.

"Very well," Mora said. "Who are your friends?"

"They are three *Norte Americanos,* sir."

"I see."

"They asked me to bring you to them."

Mora glanced at Eva. "I think it would be better to bring them here. Nothing can be done outside the city. And here I have my group to help whatever it is they must do."

Fortun nodded gravely. Mora was unshaven, dressed like a campesino. His hair was long and he looked exactly like an ordinary worker . . . which undoubtedly was his camouflage.

Mora smiled. "They will be safe here," as if Fortun had asked the question.

Fortun looked at the room, and Mora said, "There are other rooms. We can put up a dozen here."

"Jorge is right," Eva said. "We will bring them here."

"Tonight," Mora replied.

* * *

They waited till long after dark, then Eva drove down the alley and back across the city and outside it to park the car near the wide ravine. Fortun got out and went alone, whistling, walking across the field toward the hiding place. He halted when Hog's voice said, "You alone, tiger?"

Fortun slid down into the ravine. "No. There is a woman with me."

"Of course there is," Hog said, slapping his back. "She in yore pocket, huh?"

Stone said, "Start at the beginning, shortstop. Did you find Mora?"

He told the story quickly, the meeting with Roberto, then Eva, and finally Jorge Mora in the old factory. "He says it is better if you come there."

"Probably right," Loughlin agreed.

Hog asked, "There's really a girl waitin' out there with a car?"

Fortun nodded.

"Well, damn me. Let's go chop, chop." He regarded Fortun doubtfully. "But she's a big fat one, right? Tits like watermelons?"

"She is not! She is beautiful."

"Get your gear," Mark said. He slung his AK over his shoulder and climbed out of the ravine.

Damn! She *was* beautiful. Fortun hadn't told half of it! She stood by the little car, waiting for them, shaking her head at the sizes of them. Fortun introduced her. "This is Eva . . ."

They said their names, staring at her, the first pretty girl they'd seen in a while. Loughlin said, "Can we all get in that bug?"

Hog opened the door. "It's gonna flatten the tires!"

Eva said, "Two in the back with Fortun, one in front with me."

They did as she said, and Mark squeezed in the front when all were settled. "Is it far?"

"A few miles," she told him and started the engine. She gave him the silenced pistol. "If we are stopped by the police, you must use this, or we all go to the carcel." She looked at him. "I am serious."

He could see it in her eyes, she *was* serious. He said, "Of course." It looked, in the gloom, like a homemade silencer. It was on a Spanish 9mm Astra. He rolled down the side window, glancing at her sidelong.

They went by narrow unpaved streets, moving slowly, crossing busier streets with bursts of speed. The little engine chugged mightily, pushing them along. Mark thought she was taking them a roundabout way, but he made no comment.

They had just crossed a paved boulevard when Eva said, "A jeep turned with us." In a moment she said, "It's an army car." She glanced at Mark. "Slide the pistol onto my lap."

He did as she said. Hog growled, "We got four grenades left . . ."

"No noise," Eva warned. "They are coming up close now."

The jeep appeared on the left, close to them. Two men were in it, one with an automatic rifle pointed in their general direction. He called, "Stop the car."

Eva smiled at him. "Of course, senor." She applied the brakes and the little VW stopped, the jeep only a yard away.

Eva said sharply, "Senor?"

The men looked at her and she extended the silenced pistol and fired five times. Both *soldados* crumpled.

Quickly Eva put the VW in gear and moved away, turning into the next street. Stone let out his breath.

"Holy Christ!" Hog said. "You're a ring-tailed terror, missy!"

She said, "It had to be done."

Mark took the Asta from her and reloaded it.

Minutes later she turned into the dark alley and stopped before the doors. Stone got out and opened them, and she drove through and killed the engine.

They extracted themselves from the little car, stretching and looking about. Mark closed and barred the double doors and Eva banged on the pipe again.

Jorge Mora was waiting for them in the room above. They shook hands, exchanging names. Mora asked, "Did you have any trouble?"

Mark looked at the girl. She shrugged slightly, "No, not very much."

Fortun said, "She killed two policemen!"

"It was necessary. They had stopped us." She looked annoyed.

Mora sighed and nodded. "With the silenced pistol?"

"Sí," she said.

Mora had food set out for them, with coffee heating on the small stove. There were no windows in the room; they had been boarded up with plywood, but a fan in the ceiling exhausted the humid air.

As they ate, Fortun explained that he must return to the hills. He had done what he had come to do; now Captain Ortega would want him back. Eva said she would drive him to the outskirts in the little car.

When he was ready to go, Mark said, "We appreciate it, shortstop."

"Put a gold star next to your name," Hog told him. "You're a honorary Texan, boy!"

Fortun laughed and Loughlin said, "Don't take that lightly. He means it."

"I'm honored." Fortun shook hands all around. "Good luck."

Eva put the pistol in her belt, and they went downstairs to the car.

When they had gone, Mora said, "I am in communication with several people. Nobody knows where the

C.I.A. men are being held." He paused. "But we are positive General Perez knows—Colonel Haskins told you this, I am sure."

"Yes, he did. Will it be difficult to get to General Perez?"

Mora shook his head. "I think it is impossible. But of course no one has tried it. It is exceptionally difficult because no one knows exactly where General Perez is."

"We were told he has an estate here," Mark said.

"That is true. But he also has one, or a villa, in a small town not far from the city, on the lake. Many affluent people live there, or have second homes there."

"Does he have an office?"

Mora spread his hands. "He has several, depending on things we know nothing about. We have never been able to keep track of his movements because he comes and goes in a private helicopter, and we have no such vehicle. He can be halfway across Nicaragua before we are aware he has gone."

Hog commented, "Folks has habits."

"Yes. We know that Perez likes to stay at Tela. He has several boats and is a boating enthusiast. He is also very fond of giving extravagant dinners or parties. He considers himself an international playboy. Some of his friends are movie stars, you know."

"I suppose he collects things?"

Mora shrugged. "I do not know. Senoritas, perhaps. He has been seen with a hundred different women—"

"He is not married?"

"Oh, yes, he is married. But those bonds are apparently very fragile, or elastic. His wife lives at the estate here in the city and apparently never goes to Tela."

"Children?"

"He has two boys—young men. One is in the army and the other is always close to Perez. We suspect that Perez does not trust many and that his son handles his affairs."

"And Perez himself . . . is he a brain or a politician?"

Mora smiled. "From all we know, he is a politician." He went to a wooden cabinet in a corner, opened a drawer, and flipped through a number of folders, then turned back, handing Mark a photograph. "This is Perez."

Mark showed the others. They saw a head shot of a good-looking man in uniform. He was gazing past the camera in a rather theatrical pose. He had straight brows, a slightly aquiline nose, and a heavy chin. He wore a carefully clipped mustache and a tailored smile. The photo was obviously one taken for publication.

Hog said, "Looks like this feller's got the world by the balls."

"Well," Mora said with a sigh, "as far as Nicaragua is concerned, he has. He is a very rich man, of course; his family has always been immensely rich. They were able to send Perez to the finest schools—where he was an indifferent student."

"Why did he choose the military?"

"I have no idea. Apparently it appealed to him, or perhaps the uniform appealed to him. He is somewhat of a showman, you know. I mean, he poses and struts. And the military has given him what amounts to a private army. His men wear a special patch and are specially picked. You will have your work cut out. It will not be easy to get near him."

"Is he always surrounded by his guards?"

Mora shrugged. "There have been attempts on his life in the past, though none recently. Since then Perez has taken extreme precautions."

"Gun shy," Loughlin said.

Mora smiled. "It is said he wears a bulletproof vest at all times."

"We don't want to kill him," Stone remarked. "We just want to discuss a few things with him. In a friendly tone."

Mora got out a bottle, looked at it critically, and set it

on the table. He found glasses and lined them up. "No ice, I'm afraid." He poured into the glasses. "Your mission is to find out where the C.I.A. agents are held . . .?"

"Yes. And get them out if we can."

"General Perez is not the only one who knows. I am sure his chief aide, Colonel Villela, knows as well. Several others may know."

"Could we get to Villela easier?"

"I cannot tell you. We know that Villela is well guarded also." Mora pushed the glasses toward them. He picked one up and held it out. "To freedom!"

They clinked glasses and drank.

Chapter Thirteen

Lieutenant Paco Suran was not the luckiest of men. He was smart, industrious, and had a measure of imagination, but he had failed to find the *Norte Americanos*. Nothing had come of his investigation of the Ford truck and now the debacle at the airstrip defeated him. He had been positive the three fugitives were behind it, but they had disappeared into thin air.

He began to be equally positive they had help. They had swept over the airfield, completely destroying six valuable aircraft, and had killed seven men and wounded six others. A jeep had also been smashed up. How could three men do so much damage without help? And disappear into nothingness?

Worst of all he had to report that he had not caught them. He had to admit he was nowhere near catching them. He had no clues, except his conviction that they were headed for Managua. And he knew that if they got into the capital he had lost.

Major Rosas could not contain his venom. Paco was an idiot who could not catch a common cold. He could not catch the clap from the lowest *puta* in all Central America . . . no, the world!

Major Rosas did not hesitate to say that he himself was on the griddle because he had sponsored the stupidest of worms, Paco Suran, and believed in him enough to tell his superiors that the three *Norte Americanos* were as good as in the carcel. "How does that make me look! Idiot!" Rosas shouted on the telephone. "You are recalled! Bring your men back here instantly!"

Rosas would have had Paco shot if that were possible.

Instead he contented himself with distributing the men into their various units. But he saved the best for Paco. There was a microscopic station on the far Mosquito Coast, where the humidity was intolerable and the rainfall the heaviest in all the known world, and Paco was sent there.

He could reasonably expect promotion about the time Halley's comet returned. But not if Rosas was still alive.

Jorge Mora was able to get a few newspaper clippings of General Perez' estate on the edge of the city, but they were not very helpful, having been taken for different reasons than military ones.

Stone put on a disguise, a black mustache and dark glasses, and in Eva's little red beetle drove past the estate with Eva at the wheel. Unfortunately, there was little to see. The entire compound was walled and there were six guards at the fancy wrought-iron gate.

Even driving past the gate they could not see the house itself. They had only a glimpse of a curving tree-lined drive and of much shrubbery.

The guards stared at them and Eva smiled.

Stone said, when they were past, "No telling what's inside that wall. Maybe dogs."

"Oh, yes, probably dogs," she agreed.

"I wonder if it would be possible to get a plan of this house and grounds—and Tela, too."

Eva made a face. "I'm sure that is impossible. Perez is not stupid."

Stone sighed. "Yes, I suppose not."

Eva looked especially beautiful this morning, he thought. It was difficult for him to reconcile the so-sharply-etched picture of her this lovely morning with that of the night before—as she had extended the silenced pistol and pumped five shots into the two soldiers. Could she be the same young woman? He looked at her fingernails. They even had red polish on them.

To be a hunted rebel in a city full of enemies could not be a piece of cake. They had sat in the little factory room and listened to the terrible stink on the radio when the two bodies had been found. Men in high places had shouted. Further curfews had been announced, a hundred people rounded up . . .

It was prudent to go past the iron gates only once in the red VW. Too much curiosity might bring questions, and questions might well bring jail.

He asked her why she kept it red.

"Because red is black at night. Red is also a popular color here, too." She gave him a sidelong look. "But sometimes we paint the car another color with a paint that washes off easily."

"It confuses witnesses?"

"*Sí*. It does."

He asked, "You say you came from the mountains. Why are you here in the city?"

"My aunt died not long ago, and I came to her funeral. I had not been in the capital for a very long time, so I have stayed a bit. I will go back soon."

"You are not married?"

"No." She sighed. "I was betrothed, but he was killed a year ago fighting the Sandinistas. So I have taken his place, doing what I can do."

"I imagine that's quite a lot."

"It is not as much as I would like to do." She smiled at him. "I envy you your strength."

She drove back to the old factory, taking a roundabout course as usual, watching in the rearview mirror. Finally she turned into the alley, and Stone jumped out to open the double doors.

Stone reported what they had seen—not much. The walls would be easy to scale, but there was no way to know what was inside, dogs or more guards. Also, they could not be certain the general would be there. Too many ifs.

Jorge Mora doubted they would be able to get a plan of the estate, but he ventured the idea that it might be possible to fly over it and take photographs, though one overflight might be all that was possible.

"They would send up a jet fighter to do something serious to us."

Mark asked, "Is there a place to rent a plane?"

Mora shrugged. "I doubt it. The government has confiscated all or most of them. But I will ask my friends. We have people working in government offices who supply us with information. Maybe one of them knows about a plane."

There were half a dozen rooms adjacent to Mora's. They had once been offices and now were boarded up with plywood. They moved into the largest, and Mora produced three cots from somewhere.

They had been using the factory for almost a month, he told them, and would have to move again soon. They did not dare stay too long in any one spot. The government had spies and informers everywhere; people who, Mora said, would sell out their own mothers for money. It was another reason they used the red VW as little as possible and usually only at night. Mora was afraid someone would notice it entering or leaving the alley and investigate.

"Since you have people in government offices,"

Mark said, "it ought to be possible to get an idea of the general's movements."

"I'll pass the word," Mora promised.

Eva was able to get a newspaper each morning. For a long time they had been getting information from it. Mora said it was surprising how much could be gleaned, especially over a period of time, by careful readers. Many leaders, including General Perez, seemed to enjoy seeing themselves in the press and hearing of their successes . . . no matter how imaginary.

So it was a newspaper that told them General Perez was expected in the city in several days. Mora alerted his group and a watch was kept on the estate. But it was rumored that the general planned to stay at a hotel instead.

Mora thought it would be easy to get drawings of the hotel so a plan could be made.

But there was more to it than just reaching the general. It would be necessary to spend some time with him, because he was certain to be difficult. How would they get information from him?

"Hold his feet to the fire," Hog suggested.

Mark nodded. "Doesn't that mean kidnapping him?"

Jorge Mora took it a step further. "And when you're through with him, then what? Do you kill him? You can't let him go, or he will stop you from carrying out the rest of the plan."

"We'll have to hold him somewhere. I don't see killing him in cold blood," Mark said.

"It's going to be bloody messy to get him out of the hotel alive, mates," Loughlin said, shaking his head. "How many guys will he have around him?"

"Probably quite a few," Mora thought.

Hog offered, "We oughta have some idea where they're gonna be. Otherwise we'll be goin' in blind."

"Eva," Loughlin said.

They looked at him.

"Eva, dressed like a maid. She could get in and out and tell us where the guns are."

Mark snapped his fingers. "That'll work." He turned to her. "What do *you* think?"

She nodded slowly.

Loughlin said, "She's not fat enough. She's too goddamn pretty."

She smiled. "I can make myself look an ogre." She got up and walked across the room, partly bent over, screwing her face into a grotesque shape. They all laughed as she began to limp and drag one foot.

Hog said, "She still looks good t'me." He pretended to grab her.

That afternoon Mora received several drawings of the hotel that had been made by one of the cook's helpers, and they pored over them. The hotel was constructed very like all large hotels, with a garden patio restaurant and shops. The helper did not know on which floor General Perez would be staying. He would not arrive until the next day. The hotel had eleven floors.

"What if he's in the penthouse?" Loughlin asked. "Do we take him down eleven floors and through the lobby?"

Mark had to admit it did not look promising, no matter which floor he stayed on. More and more it seemed to be evident that they would have to squeeze the information out of him and kill him on the spot.

He had a suspicion that Jorge Mora and the girl had accepted that idea from the start. Perez would be one less enemy. What difference to kill him in a hotel room or out in the fields? The picture of Eva extending her hand with the silenced pistol came stealing into his mind again.

He saw her looking at him now and again. But hell. It was no good tangling with a woman while a job was in progress.

* * *

Late in the afternoon of the day General Perez was to arrive, Eva went to the hotel. She had rearranged her hair and wore a maid's costume under her shapeless dress. The hotel drawings showed her the servants' entrance, and she found the door unguarded. There were several empty wooden lockers in the maids' room. She folded her dress inside and quickly gathered a stack of towels and began to search the floors.

General Perez was on the fourth floor. There were soldiers everywhere. These men, she noticed, each wore a white shoulder patch indicating they were an elite unit and were assigned to Perez as bodyguards. When she attempted to enter the floor, two guards confronted her, turned her about, and patted her butt.

When Eva returned to the factory that night, she had to report that a raid into the hotel would be hopeless. "He has too many guards, all elite troops. I counted more than fifteen on the fourth floor. They were scattered along the hall, with automatic weapons. They were everywhere in the hotel."

Mora asked, "Did they take over the entire floor?"

"Yes, in that section. The hotel is built in three sections. Men were even on the roof. There was an armored car in the alley when I left, and one in the street in front of the hotel. Perez has had threats before."

"He's buttoned up all right," Stone mused. "No telling how many in the rooms with him. The first shot would probably bring a hundred guys."

"Bloody bad show," Loughlin remarked. "It wouldn't be so hard if we just had to smear the bloke."

Hog nodded. "We could get him from a window."

Stone shook his head. "We can't kill him, we have to question him. That means we have to have a certain amount of time alone with him."

"Maybe this is the wrong place, mates." Loughlin

put his feet up on a chair. "This guy lives in a steel cocoon."

"Could we maybe ambush him in his car?" Hog asked.

Mora shook his head. "They never publish his comings and goings. And we'd have to kill his guards—and maybe him."

Hog's brow furrowed. "Well, why'd he stay in the goddamn hotel anyways instead of his house?"

Mora shrugged elaborately. "We don't know. According to the newspapers he's in the city to hold meetings with the President and his advisors. I suspect that because there will be television reporters around, he doesn't want them at the estate."

"Yeh, I wouldn't," Stone remarked.

It was frustrating as hell, but Loughlin was probably right. It was the wrong place. They might conceivably get in, but the odds were against them getting out. The kicker was that they had to interview the guy, not kill him. That made it a thousand times more difficult.

"So that's it?" Hog said. "No go?"

"No go at the hotel," Loughlin agreed. "Maybe at the estate."

Stone nodded. "Or maybe this Tela place."

General Perez was on television that night. They saw it on a small black-and-white set that Mora put on the table, adjusting the rabbit ears to get rid of some of the snow. Perez was shown arriving at the hotel amid cheering people. The arrival had been carefully staged. The elite guards were out of the picture and the armored car was not shown. Perez, smiling like a politician, walked up the steps alone, and Mora remarked, "He's put on weight."

Perez made a short speech, saying all the usual things; then, with smiling waves at the crowd, he went into the hotel, gone in a glitter of ribbons and medals.

There were other items about Perez in the newspapers, but they revealed nothing. Mora's people reported that he was still in the hotel. Perez had met with the President and advisers several times. The dining room had been roped off twice so the high officials might dine in peace. It looked as if they were holding a series of discussions. A few foreign diplomats were also present.

Then, a day later, Jorge Mora received word that General Perez had just been driven, in his distinctive black-and-gold armored limousine with bulletproof glass, to his city estate.

An old man who looked like a rag picker came to the factory asking for Mora. "He went this morning."

"Did the guards go with him?"

"Two carloads as usual." The old man sat down. "Of course there are guards at the estate."

"How many?"

"We think about twenty." He looked around at them. "There are dogs, too. Big black ones."

"Is there a barracks inside the walls?"

The old man nodded. "The guard is divided into three shifts. About eight men are on duty at a time. The general's wife is there, too."

"How do you know this?"

"We have seen her." The old man smiled. "And one of her maids reports to us. Unfortunately, she can only get out of the place once a week."

"Where are the barracks?"

"Near the front gate, a long, low temporary building that is very ugly."

Mora thanked the man and let him go. He then translated the old man's words for them, and Loughlin grinned. "Maybe we'd only have to contend with ten men."

"And the dogs," Mora reminded them. "They'll be savage."

"Lemme borrow that silenced pistol," Hog said, "and you can leave the dogs to me."

Chapter Fourteen

One of Mora's group had stolen a battered truck. They met it on another street and piled in with Mora, Eva, and two youngsters who were armed to the teeth, gazing at the three *Norte Americanos* with round eyes. Stone wondered what they had heard.

A bearded young man drove the truck, traversing the city using byways and alleys till Stone was lost, not even sure of directions. Mora said that the police would stop and question them if they were seen. A truck at night, full of men, would be extremely suspicious. It was quite a trick to go through the city without being seen.

The truck halted in an alley alcove some distance from the estate. They would have to walk the rest of the way, going by ones and twos.

Jorge Mora led them to the wall. Two other members of the underground group were waiting with wooden ladders, flashing white teeth in the darkness as they stood the ladders against the wall. Stone saw it was made of smooth stone blocks and was about eight feet high. A third member of the group was sitting atop the wall, keeping watch. He grinned down at them.

Mora said to them, "Run to this place if you have to

come out in a hurry. We will have the ladders down on the inside and we will give you covering fire."

"Gotcha," Hog agreed.

Stone asked, "Is there a patrol outside the wall?"

"Yes, but we will be watching. They patrol in a jeep about once an hour." Mora spoke softly to the man on the wall, and he answered, *"Es OK."*

Loughlin tested the rungs and went up slowly, as if fearing they would break under his weight. He swung over the wall and dropped to the ground on the other side. Hog was close behind him and Stone followed.

When Stone dropped to the ground, Loughlin had already moved out, the silenced pistol ready, looking for the expected dogs. Loughlin moved to the left, Hog to the right—and hissed.

Stone went to one knee. He saw the dogs pass a lighted spot, several blurs of motion, silent and savage.

He heard Hog's pistol *phut, phut, phut* . . . and he had an instant to aim at the snarling dog racing at him.

He fired four times and had an impression of slavering jaws and wild eyes. The animal bucked in the air and brushed against him as Stone slid to one side.

The dog was dead as an iron mule.

It was over in seconds. There had been four dogs. Hog had accounted for two, he and Loughlin one each. No alarm had been raised. They dragged the dogs to a clump of shrubbery and left them.

There was a brick building to the right with several floodlights illuminating it. Probably servants' quarters, Stone thought. There were no lights on inside that he could see.

They skirted the lighted areas and came to a wide pool with a multitude of white chairs and tables with colored umbrellas. The pool had a high diving board and a metal-framed canopy that was apparently devised to keep the sun off part of the pool. The estate house sat behind the pool, huge and glassy-eyed, with dim lights on somewhere in the interior.

"Some folks know how to live," Loughlin commented. "That pool's big enough to have an island in it."

Stone studied the house. It was two stories—but where was the general's room? None of the windows at the back of the house was lighted. Was he sleeping with his wife? How many guards in the house? Too many questions.

Loughlin said, "Sssssh," and they dropped to the grass behind a row of flowered shrubs.

Two guards came around the far side of the house, talking in low tones. One stopped by the pool to light a cigarette. They stood a few moments, one gesturing, then they both laughed as if at a joke. Then they went on slowly and disappeared around the house.

Stone got up quickly and hurried across the open space between the house and pool, in the direction the guards had come from. Hog touched his arm and pointed upward. There was a portico or deck there. They might get into the house that way.

Loughlin had gone ahead. He came back in a moment, grinning. He beckoned and they followed him, and he showed them a ladder. Beside it was a stack of red tiles and some sacks. To the right, on a grassy plot, was a large square box that was used for mixing mortar. In it were two shovels.

Loughlin said softly, "Somebody's fixing the roof."

The ladder was leaning against the building, and Stone went up it without hesitation, Hog at his heels. He went up two stories and stepped onto a slanting roof that was covered with canvas and tacked down. Hog's knife ripped a long slit in the canvas, and he pulled it away, exposing an attic. A flashlight showed them a shallow area only about four feet high, sloping down to inches. There was a panel door to the left.

Loughlin pointed to himself and motioned to the

door. He stepped down onto a ceiling joist and, walking carefully, moved to the door with Hog behind him.

Stone stepped down, waiting as Loughlin opened the door a crack, looked back at them, and shook his head.

There was no one in the room. He stepped through.

They were in a dark upstairs room that was apparently used as a catchall. It was filled with boxes and trunks and even several large nailed-up crates. Hog went to the door, turned the knob, and looked out. He closed the door and whispered, "It's a hallway."

Music was playing from somewhere, they could hear it only faintly. Stone said, "We've got to look in all the rooms. He could be anywhere."

"Gotcha," Hog said. He opened the door and stepped into the hall. They were in the end room. There were two doors in front of them and a stairway and a window over it at the far end. With the pistol ready, Hog opened the first door. It was a linen closet.

Stone moved past him to the next door. He put his ear close to the panel, listening. Nothing. He turned the knob silently and opened the door. The room was dark and empty. It smelled stale as if unused for a long period. There was a narrow bed, a chest of drawers, two chairs, and nothing else, very spare. Maybe a servant's room.

He closed the door and pointed to the stairs, taking a step toward them.

In that second there was a sudden clanging sound from outside. It was loud and insistent, continuing like a fire alarm, promising to wake the dead.

Stone turned. "They found the dogs."

"Shit!" Loughlin said.

"Sure as shootin'," Hog agreed. "Let's get the fuck outa here."

They would never in the world get to Perez now. The only thing was to save their skins and try another day. Stone put the pistol away and pulled the Uzi from his back and chambered a round. A little noise wouldn't matter now.

Loughlin ran to the stairway and started down. Hog paused to switch off a light. He too holstered the pistol and pulled his Uzi around.

The stairway led down to a hall. They could hear men shouting outside the house. The clamor of the alarm continued, throbbing and beating like a wild thing.

"They can hear that in Amarillo," Hog commented.

Someone opened a door away to their left and stared at them in disbelief. Hog snapped a shot at the man, a uniformed guard. It spun him around, and they heard the sounds of crockery breaking.

A second man appeared in the doorway with an automatic weapon. He fired a quick burst that raked the ceiling above them, showering them with plaster dust.

Mark fired two shots. One hit the submachine gun and spun it away from the man; the second missed him, went through the wall behind, and a woman screamed.

Loughlin called, "This way—" They ran down the hall and came to a dark kitchen. Beyond the kitchen Mark could see a wide porchlike area, also dark. Beyond it were bright lights. A man opened the door from the outside and started through. Hog fired quickly, and the man slumped and fell in a heap. A guard behind him fired, spraying the kitchen with bullets that slammed into hanging pots and clanged on metal containers.

Loughlin opened a door on their right. "This way— come on!"

It was a smallish bedroom, possibly a cook's room. There was a man in bed, staring at them with round, terrified eyes. Hog ignored him. He picked up a heavy chair and threw it through the window. Then he leaned out and fired at two floodlights, knocking them both out. The yard outside was suddenly dark. Hog changed the clip in his pistol, then jumped through the window and pulled the Uzi off his back. Loughlin and Mark followed. The wall was in front of them, about fifty yards away. There were two heavy trucks parked there, near the servants' quarters.

As they started toward the trucks several men came around the building to their right and opened fire. Bullets screamed and cracked by them, rapping into the side of the brick building. Hog halted and gave them a long burst with the Uzi. Two melted away and a third dived into the shrubbery.

But other men ran from the direction of the dark pool. Stone fired quick bursts at them, hearing them yell. One stumbled over a table and went into the pool —table, umbrella, and all.

Then he was at the wall. Bullets spanged into the gray stones—then fire erupted from its top as Mora and the others fired down at the guards. Glass shattered at the house as windows were shot out.

The ladders were there as promised, and Hog and Loughlin went up and over. Stone paused atop the wall to empty the Uzi at the trucks, smashing engines and tires. Then he jumped down.

Mora yelled, "Hurry! They'll have five hundred men here in five minutes!"

They ran toward the stolen truck.

The bearded man had the engine running. The clanging alarm was still pounding out its song as they crammed into the truck and were whirled away.

The driver took the same circuitous routes, avoiding cars and traveled streets, stopping now and then in the shadows as an automobile went by, then diving into an alley.

But despite his precautions and skill, they met the weapons carrier at an intersection.

There were three men in it, all alert, with submachine guns pointing. Probably they had been sent out to look for the raiders. One shouted to them, "Stop the truck!"

Stone hissed at the bearded driver, "Smash into them!"

The man yanked the wheel instantly, shoved on the gas pedal, and the truck slammed into the squat weapons carrier as Hog's Uzi stuttered. One man yelled out, and an AK screamed shots over their heads. The force of the collision drove the smaller vehicle sideways, skidding off the road, tilting it up.

It came down with a great thump, and Loughlin's burst cut the other two men nearly in half. The bearded man backed the truck away and hauled the steering wheel around. The truck's headlights were gone and a piece of metal was rubbing hard on one tire, making a hell of a racket.

They limped across the intersection. The engine began to steam—probably the radiator had been smashed and they were losing water fast. The driver looked around, "She ain' goin' make it, senores."

"Bail out," Stone said. "We hike from here."

They were only a mile from the old factory and arrived without further incident.

Jorge Mora poured out drinks as they sat in the boarded-up room dejectedly. They had raised a lot of hell, but they had missed Perez. Situation normal, all fucked up.

"It was a good try," Loughlin said, shrugging. "But I'm beginning to think we'll never catch this guy. He goes to the crapper with a platoon holding the goddamn paper."

"Orders is orders," Stone remarked. "But sometimes they're impossible. Is Perez the only guy who will know what we have to find out?"

"Maybe his staff," Jorge said, "and Colonel Villela."

"And they're just as hard to get to?"

Jorge nodded unhappily.

Eva watched Jorge light a brown cigar. Then she said, "What about Antonio?"

Loughlin looked at her curiously. "Who is Antonio?"

"The general's son. He knows as much as his father, and he ought to be easier to get to."

Stone perked up. "Why do you think so?"

Eva smiled. "For one thing, he's married, and he probably goes to see his wife now and then—wouldn't you think?"

Mora said, "Do you know that?"

"Well, we can find out."

Hog grinned at them. "Damn if it don't pay to have a woman around!"

Chapter Fifteen

General Romero Perez paced the room like an angry tiger. He puffed a cigar, hands behind his back, and stopped to glare at an aide, Colonel Villela. "Moscow won't tell us anything?"

"Only that Volcheck is coming, General."

"You know how secretive they are," Antonio said in a soothing tone. "But at least they told us that. He should be here in a matter of days." He was a slender young man in his mid-thirties and looked very much as his father had at that age. He had the Perez eyes, everyone said, and the ambition.

"We don't need him," Perez growled, pacing again. "The advisers are a collection of fools. They would expect to get milk from a wooden cow." He pointed to Villela with the cigar. "I will send for you later."

The colonel nodded, rose, and went to the door quickly. When it closed behind him, Antonio said, "Don't upset yourself, Father. What can we do about it?"

"Protest, protest, protest. If we allow those damned Russians to rule us—" He shook his head and threw up his arms. "Then we are finished. They will push us around with their toes. El Presidente thinks that will never happen, but I have seen it happen other places. Look at Cuba!"

"Do you want to throw out the Russians?"

Perez halted and puffed the cigar, then looked at the glowing end. "I ask myself that question. We need their supplies, the things we cannot get from the *Estados Unidos*. But we do need their advice? Do we need people like Volcheck?"

Antonio lit a cigarette. "What is it about Volcheck?"

Perez gazed at his son. "Public relations."

"What?"

"They say that we military men are crusty and unfeeling. That we do everything according to the rules and regulations." He touched his temple. "But some of us can think, too. What if the world learns about Volcheck?"

"Learns what?"

Perez leaned forward. "That he is a torturer."

Antonio was astonished. "How do you know this?"

His father smiled. "I have ways." He rubbed two fingers together. "Money loosens tongues as well as anything. Yes, Volcheck will come here to torture the C.I.A. men, and if we permit it and the world press learns of it . . ." He shrugged. "We might never overcome it. They would brand us as barbarians."

"They would jump at the opportunity."

"Yes. And those stupid advisers will allow it. They will not listen to me."

Antonio was silent for a moment. He smoked absently, then stubbed the cigarette out. The *Norte Americano* agents must be interrogated, but not killed by torture. If *that* news was broadcast, the *Estados Unidos* would surely land troops and invade Nicaragua. That was what his father feared.

It had happened before.

Perez said suddenly, "How many were killed last night?"

"Five. And four more wounded. The attackers got clean away. We think they also killed three militiamen in a weapons carrier when they left here."

Perez shook his head. "Guerrilla tactics. How can we guard against them?"

"It is very difficult. They strike targets of opportunity." He glanced at his father. "We think they came here to kill you."

"Yes, I know." Perez made a face. "I could give them a list of men to attack. . . ."

"Will you stay here tonight?"

Perez shook his head. "I will go to Tela this afternoon."

"Do not drive . . ."

"No. I will go in the helicopter. When is the baby due?"

Antonio smiled. "In two or three days. You will be a grandfather."

Perez smiled broadly. "Let me know instantly."

Emilio Diaz squinted his eyes watching the helicopter land. It disappeared inside the estate walls, and he saw the dust kick up . . . then dissipate. He put down the binoculars and rubbed his eyes. He lay on a flat roof only half a block from the walls. There was a makeshift roof above him, covered with tar paper to keep out the rain or sun, and there was a trapdoor at his back that led down into the house.

He and several others took turns watching the compound. They relayed what information they gleaned to Jorge Mora. Emilio and his friends were too old to go charging about the countryside fighting the Sandinistas, but they did what they could. It was their bit for freedom.

From his vantage point Emilio could see the wrought-iron front gate and the guards. And often, through a telescope, see who came and went. Mora wanted this information.

A closed car came from the estate. The guards opened the gate for it and one saluted. Emilio trained the binoculars on it but could not see who was inside. Some cars had some kind of dark glass on the windows.

He called down to his grandson, Jaime, who was twelve. "Tell Jorge that a helicopter came. I think El Presidente was on it. Ask someone the time."

"*Sí*, Grandfather."

Jaime got on his bicycle and pedaled off at once. He stopped by a row of shops to ask a man with a wristwatch the time. The man was astonished that a small boy in tattered clothes needed such information.

When he got to the old factory, Jaime delivered his message, and Mora thanked him. Upstairs Mora said to his three guests, "Perez' helicopter just landed in the estates grounds. We think it brought El Presidente and that Perez will go with him to Tela."

"Is that common?"

"*Sí*. It has happened many times."

"And will the son go with him?"

Mora shrugged. *"Quien sabe?* Who knows? We will wait to hear again from Emilio."

It was after dark before Jaime came to the factory again. The helicopter had flown. Emilio was sure it contained Perez. He had probably gone to Tela.

"And probably Antonio with him."

"*Sí*. Probably."

Emilio Diaz and his friends had been asked to determine where Antonio Perez lived . . . specifically where his wife lived, and if possible to discover whether Antonio and his wife were on good terms. Did he visit her often?

Emilio was in bed sleeping, and Esteban Viader lay on the flat roof with the telescope when the limousine came through the wrought-iron gates of the estate.

Antonio Perez was in the back. Esteban saw him clearly in the glass. He yelled down into the house at once, and Jaime and another boy, Angel, thirteen, hurried out to follow the car. Jumping on their bicycles, they pedaled furiously. The lost the limousine once and found it again as it made a turn ahead of them, then was slowed by narrow streets for two short blocks. It entered an exclusive part of the city, and the boys lost it on a hill. When they walked the bikes to the top, it had disappeared.

"Separate," Angel said. "You go that way, I'll go this."

They rode along half a dozen winding roads, the home of affluent people who preferred the cooler air of the hills to the humidity of the city. Jaime was tired and about to give up when he saw the grille of the limousine, half hidden by shrubbery. It *was* the same car! Laying the bicycle down, he crept to the ornate fence and peered through the leafy tangle—it *was* the car!

Heart racing, he jumped on the bicycle again and rode down the hill to report.

Stone listened as Jorge Mora related what the boy had seen. He asked, "Can you watch the house?"

"That is being done."

Loughlin scratched his chin. "I thought Antonio was his old man's keeper . . . I mean, the only one the general trusted. How come Perez flew off somewhere and the son stays here?"

"Family fight," Hog said. "The old man got pissed off, kicked the kid in the ass, huh?"

Mora shrugged.

"How big is the house?" Stone asked. "Lots of servants?"

"It is a small mansion, senores. Perez and his family are very rich. They have been stealing from the treasury for generations. I cannot tell you without a report, but I would imagine there are many servants."

"How many is many?"

"Perhaps five, maybe six. And also guards. The

driver of the limousine is a soldier, one of the elite guards. Usually there is another beside him in the front, well armed despite the car's armor. There may be another two guards at the house beside them."

"Four in all."

"Yes. At least four. They probably have a guardroom in the house, where they sleep."

Stone nodded. "What about an airplane? You were hoping—"

"It is impossible." Mora shook his head sadly. "There is no plane available without many government papers and rubber stamps. We could not qualify. Our friends tell me to forget it."

"Damn," Loughlin said. "We'll have to go in blind again."

"Can we get a look at the house?" Stone asked. "Are there grounds around it?"

"I will ask my friends to take you there—but at night." Mora paused. "You will not be able to stop near the house—the guards will be very suspicious because of the raid on the Perez estate."

"*Comprendo,*" Stone said. "We can see a lot with one look and three pairs of eyes."

Another truck was stolen, and the three *Norte Americano* met it at midnight away from the factory. The driver was another of Mora's group and very young, barely out of his teens, named Paulo. He grinned at them, saying, "No speak—" He shrugged. "No *Inglés.*"

"OK," Loughlin told him. "Drive the lorry, chum."

He knew exactly where to go and took them by a roundabout course that avoided busy streets and traffic. In the hills he slowed and drove the hill roads very carefully, looking at each house. When they came close to the Perez villa, he pointed. "*La casa.*"

They drove past slowly. The house was set back from the street. It had a circular drive in which a green car was parked under floodlights. The house was apparently stucco over stone with a jungle of vines and plants and a chain-link fence with two strong-looking gates. They saw no guards. The house was not close to its neighbors and was on the side of a gentle slope with a number of trees.

Hog said, "Get over that fence easy. You figure it's electrified?"

"Hope not," Loughlin replied.

"Big question," Hog said. "How d'we get away afterwards? I mean, if we raise hell by shooting the place up?"

"We use the silencers," said Loughlin.

Stone nodded. "So we mail the guards some silencers? Listen, we've got to get in and out without firing a shot. Otherwise the damn militia will cover us like chocolate cream on a cookie."

"Things get harder," Hog complained. "We had it easy in Nam. Why the fuck we take on a job like this?"

"Because no one else could do it."

Hog sighed deeply. "No one else was dumb enough."

Loughlin said, "Could we get in, grab Antonio, and get out again with him?"

"That'd be ideal," Stone said, nodding. "Let's do it that way." He looked at them meaningfully. "And let's do it tonight."

In the upstairs factory room they discussed it with Mora and Eva. They still had the stolen truck, Mora told them. Paulo or another would drive them there and wait for them. "How long will you be inside the house?"

"Maybe five minutes," Stone said. "Maybe less. We'll cut the telephone wires as we go in so they can't call for help."

Hog rapped his knuckles on a table. "What's this bugger look like? Antonio?"

Jorge Mora had pictures of him, cut from newspapers. He passed them around. Antonio was a good-looking young man, trimmed mustache, glasses, a college man. He had gone to school and graduated from a California law school. His wife was from Managua and they had been married only about a year.

They cleaned weapons and discussed their roles in the light of what they knew or could guess about the house. In the afternoon a man on a bicycle came into the alley with a battered paper sack, leaving it at the door. It proved to be full of uniforms that had been liberated from Sandinista soldiers. A few had bullet holes. They were able to find some that fit.

In the paper sack was also a note to Mora. It had been learned, the note said, that Antonio's wife was pregnant and was expecting her child any day. There was an ambulance waiting, on call.

Mora said to them, "That's why he didn't go to Tela with his father."

It seemed a likely answer. And the ambulance would take her to the hospital to have the child.

Eva was certain about it. There was, she said, an excellent hospital in the city.

"Damn!" Stone swore. "Then Antonio will go with her!" The entire thing was getting complicated. But—if they had to, they could take Antonio off the ambulance. Maybe. How many guards would accompany it?

"Wait a minute," Stone said, facing them. "We have to go ahead with the plan as discussed. She may not have the baby for a week. And anyhow, if we have to change plans in the middle of the stream—we've done it before."

Loughlin offered, "Best tell Jorge to get someone to drive the truck who's fluent in the Queen's tongue."

Everything was ready. They would enter Antonio Perez' house with the silenced weapons and back-up pistols. Their biggest weapon, of course, would be surprise.

Chapter Sixteen

The truck, driven by the same bearded man, who spoke English, took them to within a hundred yards of the hillside mansion. It was just past midnight. The truck went on past the house and parked another hundred yards away to wait.

They had brought mats to lay over the chain-link fence, which had ugly points along the top.

They were over the fence, along the side of the house, in moments. Loughlin had noted the telephone wires and quickly cut them.

The ambulance was still waiting in front of the house. They were in luck, Stone thought. The baby was working for them so far. Stay in the womb where it's warm, kid.

It was a very large house and on one side were garages. Stone peered through a window, seeing nothing. Dark as the inside of a mule. He pulled tape from a pocket and laid it crisscross on the glass, then shoved his elbow through, pulling out most of the glass to toss into the shrubbery. He picked out the shards, then Hog hoisted him up and he was inside, stepping on a long bench, then to the floor beside a big sedan.

In a moment he pulled the bolt on a door, and Loughlin and Hog came in.

It was a three-car garage containing the sedan and a smaller sports model that, in the gloom, looked like a Porsche. On the far side was a door into the house. Hog took a moment to let the air out of two tires so neither car could be used to pursue them quickly. Loughlin cracked the door open an inch. On the other side was a hall and to the right the main entry to the house.

He closed the door and whispered, "Two guards in the entry."

"Doing what?"

"Sitting. They look half asleep."

Stone said, "They have to go."

Loughlin nodded. He stepped quietly into the hall with the silenced pistol pointed.

One guard looked up in astonishment as he fired: *Phut, phut.*

The second guard never knew what hit him.

They entered the hall as Loughlin switched magazines. Stone led toward the back of the house. Where would the wife's bedroom be? Probably upstairs. The stairs were to the left and he turned that way.

A voice said, *"Que quiere usted?"*

Stone looked around in surprise. A guard had appeared from a room on their right, obviously startled to see men in uniform, and even more astonished to see they were not Nicaraguan.

He dug for the pistol on his hip, and Hog shot him through the cheek. Blood spattered the wall as the guard slid to the floor.

But he got off one shot into the floor.

And it sounded like doom in the confines of the hall.

"Jesus!" Loughlin said. "That'll bring the bloody marines!"

"Rear guard, Hog," Stone said and dashed up the stairs with Loughlin. A man came from one of the rooms as they raced up. The man was in striped pajamas and had a Colt pistol in his hand. He started to raise it, then saw the two silenced pistols pointed at him.

Stone said, "Drop it."

Antonio was astonished. "You speak English!"

"Of course. Get your pants on. You're coming with us."

The Colt thudded on the carpet. "Going with you?"

"We're not going to kill you," Stone assured him. "Get your pants on." He picked up the pistol and shoved it into his belt. He followed Antonio into the bed-chamber, pushing the silenced Walther in the other's back. Loughlin stood at the door.

It was a plain room with a single bed. There was a dresser with a ticking clock, an open closet, and two chairs. Stone asked, "Where's your wife?"

"You're not going to hurt her?"

"Of course not."

Antonio pointed. "In the next room." He pulled his pants on over the pajamas.

"Grab a coat and let's go."

Antonio picked a coat off a hanger and went out, holding it. Stone shoved him down the stairs. "Hurry—"

Hog said, "Somebody turned lights on in the front."

"Side door," Stone said to Antonio. "Quick. Where is it?"

Antonio pointed. They went that way. The door was off a laundry room, and as they opened it, lights went on overhead. Stone paused. "Hog—get the lights."

Hog slid out, looking in all directions. The pistol coughed and the lights shattered. Glass tinkled into the shrubs. And from the front of the house someone shouted.

"Over the fence," Stone said. "Terrance, you first."

They ran to the fence as someone shone a flashlight in their direction. Hog stopped, extended the pistol, and fired three times. The light went out. Then he jumped to the fence and rolled over, grabbing the mat off, tossing it into the darkness.

They hurried down the street to the truck and piled in, Hog and Loughlin in the back with Antonio. They covered him with blankets as he protested.

Hog said, "Shut up. We ain't hurtin' you none."

They had done it.

They took him blindfolded to the old factory and sat him on Mora's couch. With Mora and Eva out of the room, they removed the blindfold.

Antonio rubbed his eyes and stared at them. "Who are you?"

Stone said, "We have some questions for you."

"I cannot answer any questions."

"Well, of course, that's up to you. But we are serious and in somewhat of a hurry. We don't want to hurt you, but if it comes down to it, we will have to."

Antonio looked from one man to the other and sighed deeply. "What kind of questions?"

"We want to know where the *Norte Americano* C.I.A. agents have been taken and held."

"Ahhh," Antonio said, nodding his head. *"That* is it."

"Yes. That is it."

"Why do you think I would know?"

Stone said, "You have put us through a lot of trouble. Let's not fence with answers. We know you have them. Where are the agents?"

Antonio looked at the floor. "And if I tell you—then what?"

"You will be held here until we find out if you have told us the truth. But if you give us trouble, we will not tell your wife that you are alive." Stone smiled. "You might not be."

"And if I tell you, you will tell her?"

"Of course. We make no war on her. Did we annoy her tonight?"

Antonio nodded. "I see."

"Where are the agents?"

"Give me a moment to think . . ."

Stone sat opposite the man, waiting. Antonio looked at him, at Loughlin, and at Hog. Then he seemed to sigh again, as if he realized his bargaining position was not strong. Hog took the magazine from his pistol, examined it, and put it back in with a sharp click.

Antonio said, "They are at a camp called Lerida. It is in the jungle."

"We have a map." Stone motioned for it, then spread it out. He handed Antonio a pencil. The young man studied the map for a moment, then drew a circle.

"It is here."

"Have you been there?"

Antonio shook his head.

"What kind of a camp?"

"To my knowledge it is only a small place, but isolated. The Russians—" Antonio stopped.

"There are Soviets there?"

"I am told so."

"How many? Are they troops or advisers . . . ?"

"No troops, or very few. It is all I know."

They put him in one of the small rooms and locked the door. Mora and Eva had heard what Antonio had said. Mora told them, "I have never heard of this Lerida."

"It may be a kind of Devil's Island, stuck out in the jungle to make it difficult for anyone to escape from." Stone studied the map. "There are no roads shown near it."

Eva asked, "Is he telling the truth?"

Stone shrugged. "Probably. What would he gain—a few days? He knows we'll find out soon."

"But he gave in too easily . . . didn't he?"

Mora interjected, "He's not his father. He's not a fighter. I think he saw we had all the cards. Or all the guns."

Stone asked Mora, "Can your people find out anything about Lerida?"

Before he could answer, Eva said, "My people can. I come from that area."

"How do you get word to them?"

She smiled. "We have a grapevine, senor."

"That gal's got ever'thing," Hog said with appreciation. She batted her eyes at him.

"Then the next thing," Stone said, "is to get us out of the city." He spoke directly to the girl. "Will you guide us, beautiful?"

She laughed prettily. "Only if Hog goes with us."

Hog rolled his eyes. "Honey, I'd follow you down the barrel of a goddamn cannon."

"After that," Loughlin remarked, "he'll make you an honorary Texan."

Colonel Francisco Villela put down the telephone with deliberation, then sat a moment, looking at the opposite wall, seeing nothing. Antonio Perez had been kidnapped.

How could he tell the general? Well, Perez would have to be told. He thumped his fist on the desk. Four men killed, one wounded, and no one alive could tell him what the raiders even looked like! It had apparently been a very smooth, professional operation, and nearly silent. The wounded man had stated he'd heard only one shot inside the house, and yet they'd found three bodies there.

Was this the same group who had raided the general's estate? There were certain similarities . . . except that at the estate they were sure the raiders had come to kill General Perez.

The nerve of men who would kidnap the son of General Perez! Was it for information? Yes, it must be. What else? Antonio was really a rather shy young man, nothing at all like his pugnacious father. The general was aggressive where Antonio was reasonable.

Well, get about it. Villela pushed a button, and in a moment his chief aide came through the door, closing it behind him.

"This is confidential for the moment," Villela said. "Antonio has been kidnapped."

The aide swore under his breath. "Rebels?"

"Undoubtedly. First get me the general at Tela. I will have to inform him."

"Yes, sir."

"Then . . . I expect we will get a ransom note. Be on the lookout."

The aide nodded. "When did this happen, sir?"

"Last night. One hurt, four guards killed."

"Isn't Antonio's wife expecting?"

"That's why he was home." Villela paused. "Who would know that Antonio stayed with her?"

"Probably a dozen people, sir."

Villela fiddled with a pencil. "Ask the security people to look into it. Give them names if you can."

"Yes sir. At once." The aide went out.

He called the chief of security immediately and went to his office on the next floor. His visit was urgent and he was admitted without a wait. The chief was a man in his fifties, stout and mustached, a lieutenant colonel of long service. He was in civilian clothes. He rose at the aide's entrance and came around the desk to shake hands. "How nice to see you, Nicolas. How can I serve the general?"

Nicolas closed the door. "This is confidential, Colonel. Antonio has been kidnapped. Colonel Villela thinks it was rebels, but a professional group. They took him at his house last night."

The chief snapped his fingers. "And the guards?"

"One wounded, three killed."

"What did the wounded man see?"

Nicolas shook his head. "You'd better ask him yourself."

"Yes, I will. Has there been a ransom note or call?"

"Not yet."

The chief's brow knotted. "First an attack on the general's estate, and now Antonio has been kidnapped. Isn't that curious? Do you suppose they were after Antonio at the estate and not the general?"

Nicolas spread his hands. "This is your department, Chief. I am not a detective."

"Hmmmm." The chief went back around the desk and picked a paper off it. "By the way, I've just received a report from one of our sparrows that there is suspicious activity at an old factory building. . . ."

Nicolas waved his hand. "Put that aside. We must get Antonio back as soon as possible. General Perez will be furious! And you know his anger. . ."

The chief nodded. "I know it well."

"Then I leave it in your hands. Colonel Villela wants you to interview all those who knew Antonio was staying with his wife last night."

"She is about to have a child?"

"Yes. Antonio would have gone to Tela but for that." Nicolas went to the door. "Good luck, Colonel."

When Nicolas had gone, the chief called in Captain Reynaldo Lopes, a stocky chunk of man, brown and weathered, with big veiny hands. He handed Lopes the paper.

"This needs investigation."

"An old factory building? *Sí*, I know the place. It's been rusting for years. You think someone lives there?"

"The sparrows say so. Put it on your list."

Lopes nodded. "Yes, sir. I'll send a squad of men there."

Chapter Seventeen

It was decided they would leave the city that night, heading into the eastern mountains where Lerida was said to be. It was also decided, over Eva's protests, that the little red VW would have to be left behind. It would carry them all, as it had before, but an enemy would be instantly suspicious of a car so bulging full of bodies.

Paulo and his friends, Mora said, would steal a car to take them partway. Paulo and the bearded man were without peer when it came to making an automobile disappear.

"We will move the red VW to the new location near the machine shop," Mora said to Eva. "It will be here when you return."

"What machine shop?" Loughlin asked.

"I told you before we were intending to move from the factory. We have prepared another place in an unused machine shop a mile from here. We will move in a week or so."

Paulo appeared after dark to go with Eva, to show her where the VW would be kept. He promised to be back before midnight with a car.

They spent an hour with their packs, putting in a few

tins of food each, ammo, and necessities. It was decided
to leave the four remaining grenades with Mora. He
would have more use for them than they. Then they got
some sleep.

Stone was awakened by Mora tugging at his sleeve.
"Shhhh. Wake your friends. We may have visitors."

He pushed Hog and Loughlin and rolled off the cot
and into his pack. He slung the AK and the Uzi over his
back and drew the silenced Walther. When he went to
the door, Hog was right behind him. "What is it?" He
looked at his watch. It was very late.

"I dunno. Jorge says visitors."

Mora had Antonio, hands tied behind his back, in the
larger room, in the dark.

Hog asked, "Where's Eva?"

"Down in the lower floor, keeping watch. Come on,
follow me." He went down the steps quickly with Antonio
at his heels. When he came close, Stone could see that
Antonio was also gagged to keep him from calling out.

At the lower door Mora became a shadow. He
slipped along the wall to his right, his face a pale blur as
he turned back to see that they followed. When he
stopped, Eva was suddenly there.

"Men are surrounding the factory," she whispered.
"Paulo and I spotted them when we returned. I sent
them away."

"How many men?" Stone asked.

She shook her head.

Mora said, "We prepared for this long ago. We have
a way out. Follow me."

As he spoke there was a soft splintering sound from
behind them. Mora said, "They're coming in the door.
Get down—get down—" He pulled the pin on one of the
grenades, let the handle up for several seconds, and tossed
it.

The explosion lit up the room for a second. There
were shrieks, then an unnatural silence.

But in the next second another shadow appeared at the door and an AK burst chattered over their heads.

Hog extended his arm and fired three times with the silenced pistol. The doorway was clear.

Mora growled, "Come on, come on—"

From the far end of the huge factory room, someone fired and the shots rapped on the wall near them, stitching rows of holes. Stone aimed as carefully as he could in the dark and returned the fire, aiming at the flashes. Someone yelled. The firing grew more intense.

Stone emptied the silenced pistol and rammed in another magazine. Hog was firing to his right, and Mora growled at them, "Come on—"

Loughlin pulled the pin on another grenade and heaved it toward the end of the huge room. They lay flat as the explosion pounded the echoes—the firing suddenly stopped.

Stone said, "Let's get outa here!"

They charged after Mora and the girl. Hog pushed Antonio along and they slipped through a narrow opening into a debris-filled area. Mora winked a flashlight. "This way—"

They crossed the littered area and ducked into a low shed, and Mora's flashlight winked at them again. A board was pulled from a wall. When Stone went through, he pushed it shut again.

They were suddenly in the next street.

Someone was firing in the factory, and Hog laughed. "Hope they's shootin' at each other."

A battered truck came along the street and stopped, and Paulo grinned at them. Mora pushed Antonio into the cab and followed. The others piled in the back under a canvas top, and the truck took off.

"Slick as a greased weasel," Hog said with satisfaction.

Stone said, "Somebody knew we were in the old factory."

"The government pays hundreds of spies and informers," Eva replied. "Jorge knew we could not stay there long."

When the truck stopped again, Jorge Mora and Antonio got out and Eva slid into the cab beside Paulo. They had only a moment to say good-byes—then Paulo put the truck in gear and they rumbled on. They made a dozen turns, crossing larger streets, wound through hills, and finally stopped.

Eva got out, slinging an AK over her shoulder. "We walk from here, amigos. There are checkpoints. Paulo will have to go back."

"OK," Stone said. *"Gracias,* Paulo."

"OK," Paulo said, sticking his thumb up, grinning at them. He turned the truck around, and they watched it disappear in the gloom.

Eva seemed to know every millimeter of the hills. She led them by winding, twisting paths around a checkpoint and into the forest east of the city.

Two hours later, when they halted for a breather, she said, "We are safe now. Let us take a compass reading."

Stone quickly set a course toward the east, and they walked another hour before halting to make a dry camp.

Reynoldo Lopes, with his shirt off, stood in front of a mustachioed campesino who was tied hand and foot to a stout wooden chair. They were in the basement of the security building near the edge of the city. Lopes lashed out with a leather whip. The slash left a red welt across the prisoner's cheek.

The man moaned, shaking his head as if drowning. Lopes growled, "You are a fool! Tell me and the beating will stop."

"I have—told—you."

"You have told me only that three *Norte Americanos*

have left the city after kidnapping Antonio Perez."
Lopes cracked the whip.

Wincing, the prisoner groaned. "It is all I know,
senor."

Lopes lashed out again and blood spurted from the
red weals. "Where did they go?"

"I do not know! Maybe—to—the east."

"Why would they go to the east?"

Miserably the prisoner shook his head. "They did not
tell me."

Lopes frowned at the man, tossed the whip to an
aide, and went out and up the steps. Why would the
Americanos go to the east? To the west was the ocean.
Maybe if they took Antonio to the east it was to an
already arranged helicopter base. All of Nicaragua was
to the east. . . .

He went to a telephone and talked to Colonel Villela,
telling him what the prisoner had said. An all-out search
was ordered.

They were up at daybreak, listening to the drone of
aircraft. In an hour helicopters came beating their way,
moving back and forth. . . .

"You figure they's searching for us?" Hog said.

"They're looking for something." Loughlin squinted
at them. "How d'they know we're here?"

"Somebody talked," Stone mused. "Maybe they
think we've got Antonio Perez with us."

Eva agreed. "We must leave this area. There will be
soldiers everywhere before dark."

She led them toward the north, staying in the shelter
of the trees, lying flat when choppers came close. When
they reached a ridge in the afternoon, they could look
back with the binoculars and see helicopters landing
men. Evidently a Class A search was under way. Stone
wondered if General Perez was leading it in person. It
was likely. Chances were he'd be raging.

When they halted again in the middle of the evening,

they spread out the map in a deep ravine and, using a flashlight, decided they were some ninety miles from the circle Antonio had drawn on the map.

The area should not be lousy with soldiers, Stone offered. Who knew they were on their way to Lerida? Jorge Mora was the only other person in the world who knew—and Antonio, of course.

"What about Paulo?" Hog asked.

"He knew only that we were leaving the city," Eva told him. "But I doubt if they can catch him. He is very slippery."

The next day the forest turned into jungle. They seemed to have left the search behind as they swung east again.

Nikol Volcheck was late arriving from Moscow. His jet landed near dark and he was whisked to a hotel with his staff and briefed by several K.G.B. agents as he ate in his suite.

He grunted, hearing that the general's son had been kidnapped by guerrilla fighters. "Why did they take him?"

"We do not know. Even Colonel Villela does not know who took him or where he is now. A large-scale search is under way to recover him."

"Very curious . . ." Volcheck sipped vodka and lit a cigarette. "Is it not odd that they kidnapped him instead of simply killing him?"

"They want information from him. He is his father's chief of staff."

"Ahhhh. What information?"

His aides and the K.G.B. men shrugged. "It could be anything. It could be simply to hold him for ransom— but no note has surfaced."

"Well, that is their business. Let us get on with ours. Where are the agents being held?"

"They were taken to a base in the jungle, sir. It is a remote place—"

"But hot and humid?"

"I am afraid so, sir. Yes. It is necessary to go there by helicopter. There is a road, but it is miserable."

"Very well. Make the arrangements."

It was slow going; they could not see the sun and had to rely on compass readings. Also, it was difficult to estimate how far they had traveled. Stone feared they might go past Lerida and never see it.

"That's right," Loughlin agreed. "We might come out on the goddamn Caribbean any minute."

Hog said in a low voice, "Movement." He pointed and went to one knee, glancing at Stone. "Right through there."

"Spread out," Stone said softly. "Easy. . ." Had they met a Sandinista patrol? This was a good region for one.

Eva, beside him, whispered, "They could be Indians . . ."

They were motionless for long minutes and saw nothing more.

Stone stood slowly, his Uzi at the ready. He heard only the ordinary sounds of the jungle. When there were no sounds, that was when danger lurked.

"Keep spread out," he told them. They had probably met an Indian hunter, and he had faded into the jungle after looking them over.

Eva led them into a narrow valley that wound like a snake for several miles. They crossed a large burned area that looked, in the center, as if a huge explosion had taken place not long past. Maybe a flier had jettisoned bombs . . .

As they came out of the valley Loughlin raised his hand and sank down silently. Stone crawled to him. "What?"

"I saw someone—gone in a second—a blur of face."

"What kind of face?"

Loughlin grinned at him. "Like us, chum."

"American?"

"Well, probably Nicaraguan. That's American too, isn't it?"

"How far away?"

Loughlin pointed with the Uzi barrel. "Right along there, maybe forty feet, but gone in a second."

"Not Indian, then?"

"Definitely not a naked Indian, no. Wore a hat and shirt."

"All right. Stay low." Stone crawled to the right and lay motionless. Was someone paralleling them? Leading them into a trap?

This was a hell of a place to fight a battle, where a man could not see his enemy.

Just like Nam . . .

Chapter Eighteen

To Stone's amazement Eva suddenly stood and started singing. She went on for several moments, then there were voices in the jungle, and someone called out.

"It's my people!" Eva said, rushing forward, slinging her weapon across her back.

There were twenty or more, all dressed roughly, with weapons slung, but smiling and embracing the girl. Among them was an uncle she called Xavier. He was an older man, grizzled and stringy, with a wide smile that exposed missing and crooked teeth. He spoke English badly, and Eva translated most of the welcomes.

The group had tracked them, thinking at first they were Sandinistas, then deciding they must be rebels— but yet not sure.

They had set up a camp in a clearing and invited the *Norte Americanos* to come along. The group was traveling to meet with other rebels, Xavier told them. They hoped to cause the government some harm. Did they know of a place called Lerida? They had heard of it. None of them had been there.

Xavier gestured vaguely toward the southeast. It was

somewhere in that direction. "He says it is not a military objective," Eva explained.

"Tell him we think there are prisoners there."

The girl spoke to Xavier in rapid Spanish, and they discussed it till Xavier shook his head. Eva shrugged. "He says his group will first do what they intended. Then, later on, they will think about Lerida."

"Damn if it ain't hard to argue with that," Hog said. "The man has made up his mind."

Xavier put scouts out, and they built fires and cooked meat. There was no need for watches, so all three slept soundly. In the morning they were up at dawn, and Stone took Eva aside.

"Are you going on with us?"

She smiled at him. "Do you need me now?"

"I never knew a woman who was a bigger asset to a group. As Hog would say, you done pulled yore load."

"But I think from here on, I might be in the way."

He shook his head. "I'll never agree to that."

"Let's be serious. You no longer need me as a guide. I can tell you nothing of the land between here and Lerida. And I might be of service to Xavier."

Stone nodded. "All right. I won't forget you very soon—none of us will."

She stood on tiptoes and kissed his cheek. "Our paths will cross again, *amigo mío*."

"I hope so."

Lerida was a collection of rude huts, shacks, and buildings in a wide clearing. It was surrounded by a high bamboo fence with barbed-wire coils along the top. There had been a tower, but termites had eaten away one post and it had fallen. The post commander had decided it was not worth rebuilding.

There were four main buildings with stone foundations, and half a dozen smaller ones with none. The four had been whitewashed at some time in the past and were numbered front and back, one to four. Building number three was used as a barracks and prison. The *Norte Americanos* were in the upper room in two of the cells, of which there were five. The other three were vacant at the moment.

The walls, ceilings, and floors were of wood, but the bars were steel, brought from Managua. The jungle post, Lerida, had been used for several years as a high-level detention camp and interrogation base. Very few in the government even knew of its existence.

As a general rule, those who were sent here remained. Along the south wall of the camp was a small cemetery.

The two agents, Don Shepard and Jack Harris, were pale and looked underfed, which they were. Shepard was stocky, shorter than the rangy Harris.

The post commander, Lieutenant Tarrago, was given a pittance each month for food for prisoners. He was not expected to fatten them up, as his superior in Managua was fond of saying. Every service has its jokes.

Shepard and Harris were in separate cells, both on the same side of the room, so they could not see each other. They were able to converse—when the guard was out of the room. They were forbidden to talk to the guard or he to them, so that the guard could not be bribed.

They had reluctantly agreed, soon after they were put into the cells, that escape was impossible. They had nothing but their fingernails to use on the walls, and most important of all, they had no idea where in Nicaragua they were being held. They had been brought to Lerida at night, blindfolded.

The guards had stripped them at once, but allowed them to keep personal effects, combs, electric razors, wallets . . . Now and then one of them was taken out of the cell and allowed to plug into an electrical outlet to use his razor. Each man had been given a ragged cotton shirt and pants. No shoes. Each had also been given a collection of lice with the clothes.

Once a day they were taken into a small board-walled yard and allowed to walk about, exercise, or talk with each other... under the sharp eyes of armed guards who patrolled the walls above them.

When they had first arrived at the camp, they had protested their incarceration bitterly to Lieutenant Tarrago. He had only smiled and assured them their situation would change... very soon. He refused to elaborate on that. He also refused to allow them newspapers or current magazines.

It was a wrench to part from Eva Castelo. All three of them had accepted her so fully. She had never asked for special treatment or balked at any task they set her... and she did decorate the landscape.

When they parted, Xavier and his people went toward the west, and Eva followed. She turned back once, before the jungle swallowed her up, to stand for a moment and wave.

Stone said, "Shit."

Hog remarked to the area, "Hell, I'm glad she's gone. She was a big pain in the ass."

"Yeh," Loughlin agreed. "Always whining and bitching. Got on your nerves."

Stone rolled his eyes. "Get moving."

He set a course using the compass, and Hog led out. The jungle was not as thick and impenetrable as it would be farther east, but it was difficult.

What was ahead of them? Would there be troops at Lerida? Probably not many, the post hidden in the jungle. Perhaps there were patrols. A good commander would take precautions against a surprise raid.

They paused every hour to check the compass, and in four hours they came up against cliffs and a huge area of landslides. They turned westward and the going was even more difficult, probably the result of earthquake action centuries ago. The jungle had swarmed over it, and it seemed to take forever to get onto more or less level ground again.

They were bunched together, getting ready to climb out of a sharp depression, when Stone saw the reflection.

He grabbed Hog's belt and hauled him down, yelling at Loughlin to duck. A hail of bullets pounded and shredded the lip of the depression—exactly where their heads had been a second before.

"Thanks, neighbor," Hog said. " Damn if that ain't unfriendly."

"Sandinistra patrol, probably," Stone remarked. "Shoot first and go look later."

"This's probably restricted territory." Loughlin said, sliding the Uzi off his back. He led toward the right as Stone pointed.

The Sandinistas probably thought they were rebels. And if so, the enemy would do its best to eliminate them completely.

They made their way to the right, keeping low. In a few moments Loughlin halted, lying on his belly. He turned his head slowly and mouthed the word "grenade."

They had two left that Jorge Mora had not taken after the fight in the old factory. Stone opened his pack and pulled one out, yanking off the tape. He handed it to the Briton, pointed to the right, and Loughlin nodded. He looked back at Hog, who nodded.

Loughlin pulled the pin, let the handle up, and looped the grenade over his head in a high arc. It came down forty feet away and exploded. Then, all three got to their feet and dashed to the right a dozen yards. A burst of AK fire sprayed the ground.

Loughlin grinned. "Got three of 'em in a bunch." He shook his head. "Too bad."

They moved forward again with Stone in the lead, the silenced Walther in his hand. The jungle was suddenly quiet. He flattened himself on the earth and waited. Almost at his nose a drop of water ran down a broad green leaf and poised itself at the edge, growing fatter . . . till it dropped heavily. In another moment a second drop ran down.

Something moved just beyond a tangle of roots thirty feet away. The movement became a brown face and neck.

Stone aimed the Walther and squeezed the trigger— *phut!* The face jerked away and disappeared.

Instantly AK fire smashed into trees to their left, and leaves and bits of wood showered down. Stone fired again, guessing where the shots came from.

Loughlin and Hog crawled to the right, and Stone followed, keeping a wide interval. A grenade exploded suddenly some distance to their left, and a second grenade followed, slightly closer, then a third hit behind them. Somebody was a lousy guesser. Maybe the grenade tossers were hearing a frightened animal.

The enemy had no way of knowing how many they faced and perhaps it kept them cautious. The jungle was silent once more, and they hugged the earth. Several minutes dragged by, then suddenly there was an uproar of sound.

A dozen AK's were firing at once, pouring gouts of lead, all concentrating on an area of ground well to their left.

Stone motioned, and they rapidly moved away from the sounds. The enemy would soon discover there were no bodies in front of them, and no return fire. They'd begin to look elsewhere.

And it only took a short time. As they moved to the right, with Hog in the lead, shadows appeared not far in front of them and bullets raked the trees.

Hog replied with the silenced pistol and the firing stopped.

Then, as they continued toward the right, stray shots came seeking them. Stone fired at the sounds with the

Walther. Loughlin did the same. Automatic rounds chattered over them, and someone yelled as Stone emptied the pistol.

This was a nervous business, firing at an unseen enemy. They had to get away from these guys. Stone motioned and hissed at Hog, pointing left. If the Sandinistas thought they were moving to the right—they'd go left and double back. Fuck 'em.

Following Loughlin, they crawled to the left with bullets spanging and tearing the jungle around them recklessly.

Gradually the firing died out. There were a few sniping shots, then someone threw a granade. Finally all was still. The enemy would move forward, discover no bodies, and it might all start again.

Stone led them south once more. They could hear the Sandinistas far to their right, wasting ammunition. It would be interesting to see the report their officer made, Stone thought. He could give his imagination free rein. . . .

Nikol Volcheck was an important man, but he was in Nicaragua on a secret mission. The newspapers were not told of his arrival and he was not presented to the President. He did meet with Colonel Villela, then was driven to the airport, where a helicopter waited. He and two members of his staff were flown to Lerida.

The *Norte Americano* agents had been captured at a very opportune moment. Moscow needed information about American intentions in Nicaragua, indeed in Central America, and these agents were certain to have that knowledge.

But reluctant to give it up. So Volcheck had been dispatched to squeeze it out of them.

Nikol Volcheck's career was dotted with such missions. Because of an affair that western newsmen had uncovered despite K.G.B. camouflage and denials, a

French newspaper had referred to him as the Beast of the Black Sea. Many would agree with the title.

Volcheck was an uncomplicated man. He did not argue with or sidestep his orders. If he was told to get information, no matter how, he got it. If the victim did not recover, it was no skin off Volcheck's Soviet ass.

His helicopter landed on the jungle pad, and he was taken at once to his quarters, which were air-conditioned. The generator was fickle, but it often worked most of the day and night.

After a nap and a bath and dinner, he asked to see the two agents, to satisfy his curiosity. They were taken to a room that had a one-way mirror, and Volcheck stared at them for several moments, grunted, and walked out.

He gave orders that he would begin his interrogations the next morning.

General Perez, since the abduction, was difficult and irritable. The guards and the unlucky officer in charge at Antonio's residence had been jailed, charged with malingering and incompetence and other things. . . . The general lashed about in his anger.

Antonio's wife had given birth to a girl child two days later, which had not helped. General Perez had wished for a boy.

And, worst of all, the three damned *Norte Americanos* who had kidnapped his son had not been captured. The grand search had gone nowhere. To be sure, the searchers had turned up a number of wanted persons, but not the kidnappers.

Colonel Villela had quietly suggested that perhaps the three had taken Antonio out of the country. Villela told his wife that he would not bet a single centavo that Antonio was still alive. "They will squeeze information out of him, then kill him. Mark my words. We will find his body in a ditch one of these mornings."

But to Perez, Villela had not dared suggest that Antonio might be buried somewhere in the city or the forest. Why keep him alive to be a hindrance? And, too, Antonio might be able to point out his abductors one day. No, Antonio was long dead.

General Perez had only growled at the idea that Antonio might have been taken out of Nicaragua. "Why would they do that? They will send a ransom note soon —you will see."

"Yes, of course," Villela replied, believing no word of it.

When he got his mind off the abduction, General Perez was very interested in the Russian, Nikol Volcheck. He greatly deplored the man's reputation and despised Volcheck for it. Perez was a soldier, proud of his calling; he was a fighter, as aggressive and ruthless in battle as the next, but he was not a man to shoot an enemy in the back. He had his faults and they were legion, as his enemies could testify, but he was willing to stand and be counted.

He had certain scruples, and as he had told his son once, he had to be concerned with public relations. Too often those deep, dark secrets one wished to conceal got out into the open and were dissected by the press. Nicaragua had enemies who would like nothing better than to defame her leaders.

But especially if the Giant of the North, the *Estados Unidos,* discovered that two of its agents had been captured and tortured, Perez was convinced the Giant would invade Nicaragua.

He would do the same if the positions were reversed.

And if invasion came, then all was lost.

However, to Perez' surprise, El Presidente did not agree with him. El Presidente was commander in chief, and he asserted that Volcheck was not a torturer. Did not the Russian Embassy deny it? In fact, the Russians were insulted that anyone would think it.

General Perez stood in the palace, facing the marble

portraits by the magnificent tinkling waterfall in the reception hall. "We must expect the Russians to say that, sir."

"I am convinced they are telling the truth, Perez. Convinced. The man is nothing more than a skilled interrogator."

"I cannot believe it, Excellency. The man's reputation is blacker than sin."

El Presidente shrugged. "You listen to gossip, Perez. You know such things are not always true."

"Perhaps. But I fear we are making a terrible mistake."

El Presidente regarded him curiously. "Why do you defend the *Norte Americanos?*"

"Sir—I am defending Nicaragua!" Perez drew himself up.

"Bueno. I am delighted to hear it."

"What if the world press learns of the torture?"

"There is no torture! I forbid you to say those things! Be careful, Perez, that *you* do not spread lies."

Perez was silent a moment. "Then let me go to Lerida, Excellency. I will make a full report to you."

"You will *not* go!" El Presidente took a step forward, fists clenched. There were white spots in his cheeks. "This matter does not concern you! I have given orders that Senor Volcheck is not to be interfered with. He has my full confidence." He pointed a shaking finger. "See that you obey those orders!"

"But, Excellency! The three *Norte Americanos* who kidnapped your son are possibly heading for Lerida."

"Why should they?" El Presidente paused. "Three men? Just three? Do you panic over three men?"

"They are—unusual men," Perez said stiffly.

"You will return to Tela, General." El Presidente's tone was cold. "You will please remain there until I send for you."

* * *

They had not escaped the Sandinistas. The patrol was larger than they'd thought, and they ran into another section of it as they moved to the south. They were challenged, could not give the proper countersign, and were fired on.

Hitting the ground, Stone motioned them to the left. they must move quickly or find themselves between two fires. Several men charged them, and Stone, lying on his stomach, fired the Walther, aiming deliberately. The silenced rounds cut them down.

He reloaded, waiting for a response, and none came. Praise Allah for the silencers.

But they left a trail; it was impossible not to. They had to cut their way. It could not be helped if they were to hurry at all. Hog and Stone brought up the rear, firing at every movement. It must be disconcerting to the pursuers to see men drop and not hear shots. The return fire was usually wide of the mark. There was no sound or muzzle flash to help.

They came to another area of volcanic action. The ground was a jumble, as if some great hand had thrust up from beneath. It was covered with a tangle of growth but less thick than what they had just left. It was a place made for ambush. Silently they separated so there were several yards between them, and waited.

The pursuers appeared, moving cautiously—and were shot down, bringing bursts of AK fire that did no damage.

It was an odd battle, silent on one side, and very soon the pursuers withdrew, presumably to discuss the situation.

"They'll try to flank us," Stone said. "I vote we bug out."

They left the enemy behind and turned east again, following a deep valley with a rushing stream that they crossed on footlocker-sized boulders. As the valley broadened they turned south and just before dark came across a road.

"Hallelujah," Hog commented. "The highway to Hell."

Chapter Nineteen

It was a poor excuse for a road, nothing more than a tunnel cut in the jungle growth, a single track, a winding path, but it undoubtedly led to Lerida.

"Where else would it go?" Loughlin asked. "Maybe to the Jungle Hilton?"

The road had seen no scraper for a very long time—if ever. But it was probably easily passable to trucks. They would need more supplies and equipment at Lerida than helicopters could bring in—and troops had to be rotated constantly.

They made camp in the middle of the road, built a fire, and rested. They were all light sleepers, Loughlin argued, why keep a watch? They were in the middle of nowhere, but Stone overruled him and took the first watch. He walked down the road as they slept, thinking about Eva. He had met a lot of girls, but none quite like her. What would she be like back in the States, where people weren't shooting at each other on sight? It was impossible for him to imagine her with a baby, for instance. Well, she probably couldn't imagine him in a settled existence, either. He smiled to himself. Neither could he.

In the morning they followed the road, heading generally east and grateful for the easy going. Nothing was quite as tiring as pushing through a jungle of clinging vines and creepers. They marched steadily, and Stone wondered who had laid out the snakelike road. It must be a terrible chore keeping it open with the jungle trying to reclaim it daily.

Every hour or so they halted for a breather.

And as night fell they saw the lights behind them. They were flashing up and down as if someone were signaling.

"It's trucks," Hog said. "Headlights!"

"You bet your ass," Loughlin agreed. "And just in time, too. That's our ticket into the town."

"Right!" Stone said. "How many are there, three or four?"

"I'd guess four." Loughlin peered at them.

"Then we grab the last one—unless it's full of troops. If so, let 'em go on by."

"There's a hill up ahead." Loughlin began running. "It'll slow 'em down."

They hurried and stationed themselves, Stone on one side, Hog and Loughlin on the other.

"No shooting," Stone warned.

They ducked out of sight and waited. It was a convoy of four trucks led by an armed jeep. A tactical error, Stone thought. The jeep should have brought up the rear.

Boarding the last truck proved to be no trick at all. Stone moved out as the loaded truck labored up the hill, grinding gears. He jumped on the running board, hearing the driver yell. He shoved the .44 magnum in the man's startled face. In the next second Hog opened the door on the other side and slid in, grabbed the man, and hauled him out.

Stone opened the door and got behind the wheel. It was all done in a moment.

The truck had stalled, but Stone pushed the starter and got it going, and they chugged away after the others, leaving the driver lying in the middle of the road. He would have a terrible headache later. . . .

"Piece of cake," Loughlin said.

It was a big open-sided six-wheeler with a canvas tarp stretched over the load. They followed the truck ahead of them at more or less steady pace, bouncing and jolting over the ruts.

It took two hours to reach Lerida.

"It's not a town," Loughlin said in surprise. "It's a fort! It's got a bamboo wall around it."

The jungle was cut away from the wall about a hundred yards all around. Big floodlights were on, making the entrance as bright as day. Hog and Loughlin ducked down as they got near. Apparently some signal had been given, probably a radio in the jeep. The gates were open, and they drove through into a wide, open area.

There were several large buildings off to the right and a number of smaller ones along the bamboo wall. It was evident this was a military post; they saw no civilians at all. Lerida was a much smaller place than they'd expected.

Stone followed the truck ahead of him, and as each pulled in and backed to a loading ramp under lights, he did the same. A crew of men had already started unloading the first truck.

"OK," he said. "Nobody around. Slide out easy."

Hog opened the door and jumped down, Loughlin on his heels. Stone got down on the other side, watching the men on the ramp. No one looked their way. Two men started to pull the tarp off the next truck in line.

He joined the two others in the shadows of the building. They were in Lerida. Now where were the American agents?

* * *

Two men tied husky Don Shepard to a chair in the small windowless room. Testing the knots, they stepped back and nodded to the third man.

Nikol Volcheck lit a cigarette, pocketed the lighter, and faced Shepard. In a conversational voice he said pleasantly, "What I need from you is a complete picture of United States intentions in the Central American area. Would you prefer to dictate to a clerk, or would you rather write it out yourself?"

Shepard shook his head. "I have no such knowledge. You need to ask the ambassador."

Volcheck's thick brows rose. "Indeed? Let me make myself clearer. We are quite sure you have that knowledge and we are prepared to use any means to get it."

"How can I tell you what I don't know?"

Volcheck tapped an ash from the cigarette. "It is not my place to debate with you, Mr. Shepard. Let me tell you this: You are far from any habitation at the moment. Very far. Your government has no idea where you are and cannot help you. You are alone."

"My government knows I was captured by Sandinista troops."

Volcheck smiled. "Not so. Your government knows only that you and Mr. Harris disappeared. Unfortunately, no one survived the helicopter crash but the two of you. There is no one to tell anything. Your government will be told that bandits took you—if we decide on that course. As you are aware, it is easy to disappear forever in the jungle."

Shepard stared at the other expressionlessly. "You are threatening me with—what?"

Volcheck waved his hand. "Oh, I prefer to say I am telling you facts." He puffed the cigarette and snubbed it out. "Shall we get back to basics?" He rocked on his heels, hands in his coat pockets. "Do you wish to dictate or write it out yourself?"

"I have nothing to say to you."

Volcheck shrugged. He went to the door, opened it, and beckoned. A huge, well-muscled man in a form-fitting T-shirt entered and made a little bow to the Russian.

Volcheck said, "We will start now, Alexi."

Stone led the way around the dark building, keeping in deep shadows. At the corner he paused; apparently all the larger buildings were in the center of the wide compound. The smaller ones were lined along the bamboo wall that surrounded the project. In front of him, as he peered around the corner, was a parked helicopter. To the right of the chopper were two battered trucks painted deep green. Beyond the trucks was a canvas-covered jeep. He saw no guard near them.

But in a moment two men came along the far wall. They were talking, had slung weapons, and were obviously a perimeter guard.

Everything looked normal. The driver they had left far behind in the road had not yet been missed—at least no alarm had been raised. So far so good.

In which building were the C.I.A. men?

Hog nudged him and Stone turned. Hog extended a burly arm, pointing. "That there's a barracks, or I'm a little yeller tadpole."

Stone grunted assent. The building had a row of small windows along the side they could see. It certainly had the look of a barracks. The next building was a trifle smaller and had a large black smokestack at the far end. Could it be a workshop or a kitchen? They would need both here. It was probably a kitchen and a mess hall.

The building they stood beside was obviously a warehouse and supply depot. Looking up, Stone could see very few windows and those very small.

That left two of the larger buildings. There were lights on in one; the other was dark.

They could get to the lighted building by staying in the shadows. Stone pointed to the route and to Lough-lin. He ran quickly to the shelter of the wall. Hog waited a moment and followed. No alarm.

Stone ducked down and ran, lining up with them. Above their heads was an open window with mosquito netting tacked over it. They boosted Loughlin up to peer through. When they let him down, he said, "It looks like a rec room. Nobody in it. There's lights somewhere far back. Lemme cut the netting."

He pulled his knife and slit the netting along the bottom. This time when he looked he said, "It's a rec hall all right. The lights are upstairs."

"Let's go in," Stone decided. Maybe the prisoners were up there. They boosted Loughlin up again, and he slid through the window and pulled Hog up. Stone passed up his weapons, and they hauled him into the room. They were in a small, unlit recreation room. It had a pool table, two pinball machines, and half a dozen tables. Loughlin looked into the hall. It was dark, with a small bulb burning at the far end near a stairway.

Across the hall was a heavily screened armory room. Stone examined the lock. "Can we get into that?"

Hog said, "It'll make some noise. . . ."

"I saw some pillows in the rec room." Loughlin went back and returned with them. Hog took them, pressed them tightly against the lock with his body, and used a short, thick-bladed knife. He worked at it for several minutes, swearing under his breath. The lock was imbedded in the wood upright, and he dug the lock out completely, then yanked the door open. There was a loud splintering sound and Hog slipped inside.

Stone said, "Terrance—guard." Loughlin raised his silenced pistol, and Stone slipped into the room with Hog.

Hog asked, "What we lookin' for?"

"Flashlights—explosives—grenades—"

"Well, what about these?" Hog pulled a heavy box forward on a shelf. Stone smiled. It was a box of grenades.

They filled three gunnysacks with them and handed one to Loughlin. Stone said. "Now upstairs. See what's there."

As they came out of the room a voice called, *"Que desea ustedes?"*

A man had just come down the stairs and was standing at the end of the hall, frowning at them. Apparently he decided they were suspicious. He groped at the holster at his belt, and Hog put three shots into his chest. The man was slammed back against the wall and crumpled. Someone shouted from the stairs.

"Shit!" Loughlin growled. "The fat's in the fire!"

"The next building," Stone said. "Quick."

Loughlin ran for the door with Hog behind him.

Stone fired two shots at movement near the end of the hall and jumped outside as a hail of bullets smashed the door behind him to bits.

Almost instantly an alarm bell began to ring and the sound was immediately taken up by another bell on the far side of the compound.

Hog snapped several shots at the floodlights nearby, and they shattered, darkening the yard. The next building was smaller. Two guards came to the door, and Loughlin sprayed them with his Uzi. One sprawled on the steps, and Hog jumped over the body and yanked the door open. Loughlin instantly tossed in a grenade. Hog closed the door and stood aside as the blast thundered and smoke seeped through cracks.

Stone threw two grenades at the building they had just left. One hit the steps and exploded outside; the other went through the door, and the blast lit up the area for a second.

As he ran through the door after Hog, he saw fire gush up.

Loughlin's Uzi stuttered in the hall. There was a line of closed doors. The last one was open, shattered by the burst from the Uzi. A body lay on the floor, facedown.

Men were shouting outside. Stone guessed that no one knew what was happening or who had attacked them. The three raiders had caused pandemonium. The building they had just left was burning fiercely, lighting up the yard. That would take their attention.

He ran to the second-story steps. A man was coming down.

The Walther barked, and two shots sent the man sprawling backward. The body slipped down several steps and halted. The man's pistol bumped to the bottom.

Pausing at the top of the stairs, Stone glanced around. He was in a guardroom with steel-barred cells. This must be it! He called, "Anyone here—anyone home?"

Two voices answered instantly. "Hell, yes! Over here!"

Two men were clinging to bars in two separate cells, both grinning at him. One was stocky and one lean, but the stocky one looked as if someone had worked him over pretty good with a rubber hose.

Stone asked, "Where're the keys?"

"On the desk over there." The rangy man pointed.

Loughlin was at the top of the stairs, the Uzi ready.

Stone ran to the deck, grabbed up a ring of keys, and ran back to the cells.

The stocky man asked, "Who are you guys?"

"Friends," Stone said, trying one key after another. "Colonel Haskins sent us."

"Jesus!" the lean man said. "Haskins, huh?"

He got the first door open, and the lean man hurried out. "I'm Harris," he said, "he's Shepard."

Automatic fire chattered at the bottom of the steps. Loughlin drawled, "Can you snap it up, chums?"

The second door opened, and Stone ran for the stairs. "Come on." He dropped the keys and followed Loughlin down. Hog met them at the bottom, motioning toward the back. "There's a mob out front."

"Right." They ran to the back as Hog pulled the pins on two grenades and hurled them through the front door.

Loughlin fired short bursts at the floodlights, shattering them. "There's a jeep over there—"

Harris said, "Why not take the chopper?"

"Because none of us can fly the bloody thing," Loughlin told him.

"Well, I flew one in Nam. I think I can remember. . . ."

Bullets began to rap into the building behind them. A group of soldiers ran toward them from the right, led by a man in civilian clothes who waved his arms in anger.

"Down," Stone growled. They hit the dirt, hearing Harris say, "That's that sonofabitch Volcheck!"

The soldiers were brightly lit by the burning building. Harris had picked up an AK dropped by one of the guards in the building. He lay full length, aimed, and squeezed off a long burst.

Stone saw the shots smash into the Russian, shattering his chest.

Volcheck went to his knees, then fell on his face.

The burst also took out two soldiers near him. Hog hit one of the others and the rest scattered.

Stone heard voices in the building behind them. Turning, he flung a grenade through the door. It exploded just inside, and Loughlin rolled another down the hall. Its blast echoed and someone screamed. The building began to burn at the far end.

But the helicopter was a long way across the dark yard.

Someone was getting an organized resistance together. They heard orders shouted, and several soldiers ran from far to their right. Hog fired single rounds at them, knocking one ass over teakettle.

"Let's try for the chopper," Stone said grimly. "Terry in front—go!"

They ran a dozen paces and a fusillade screamed at them from the left. Loughlin ducked down, rolling, pulling the pin, tossing the grenade all in one fluid motion. Hog threw another and the explosions came almost together.

Someone was firing from an angle of the building far to their left. Too far for a grenade. Stone rolled, brought up the AK-47, cradling it. His burst smashed the corner, shattering the wood. He waited a few seconds and fired another.

The burning building was a torch, lighting the entire compound bright as sunlight, creating deep shadows. The second building was flaming, though they could hear frantic yells as someone tried to put out the fire.

The helicopter sat like a fat duck a hundred yards away. Could they reach it? Stone glanced to his right. The shadows were thick along the bamboo wall. Maybe that was the better route.

Somebody fired at them from one of the upper windows of the near building.

Hog rolled onto his back and his Uzi stuttered, shattered the window, and moved to the next. He shoved in a new magazine. "Let's get outa the limelight, neighbors."

Stone pointed. "Head for the wall." He began firing as they ran. Shepard hadn't moved. He nudged the man. "Get your ass in gear!"

No movement.

He looked closer. Jesus!

There was a red hole where Shepard's ear had been. The guy wasn't going anywhere.

Shit.

Stone got up and ran to join the others as Hog and Loughlin gave him covering fire. It was dark as hell by the wall, but the entire yard was bright. The fat duck stood out in bold relief.

So close and yet so far.

Could they possibly get to it, get it started, and take off before they were sliced to pieces?

Not likely.

He saw the glum looks on their faces. None of them thought they would make it.

Chapter Twenty

What other alternatives did they have? They could go over the bamboo wall into the jungle. But they had no rations now. It was obviously impossible to grab one of the trucks, as impossible as getting the chopper off the ground.

Besides, General Perez and his government troops would know where they were in a few hours—maybe someone was sending out a report this second.

The area for twenty miles in every direction would be covered. Perez would put everybody but his shoeshine boy on the line. They would all end up like Shepard.

But they couldn't sit and wait for the Sandinistas to come and gather them in. They had to try!

Stone rose, about to order them to make for the chopper—when the building blew up.

It was a tremendous, ear-splitting blast that knocked Stone on his ass and mauled their eardrums. Debris was flung a mile into the sky, raining down like a huge Fourth of July firecracker. Dazedly they slapped at the burning bits. The pyre must be visible for forty miles! It seemed the entire world had turned to fire! The heat of it seared their faces.

Stone scrambled to his feet. "Get up! Shake your asses!" He began to run for the chopper.

Lanky Harris reached it first. He grabbed the door open and piled in. Hog pushed Loughlin, and Stone was yanked in as the engine began to cough and stutter. The rotor blades began slowly to move.

They could see no one moving in the compound. Harris and Loughlin lay flat, AK's out in front of them as they scanned the area.

Hog swore steadily, clicking switches. "Come on, baby—come on—"

The blades swung faster.

Where the building had been, only the flames hissed and leapt. There was a vast blackened mess, smoking like a vision of Hell. Anyone who had been close was either dead or stunned. The second building was burning fiercely, helped by burning brands from the explosion. No one would save it. One of the trucks was also burning, and Stone could see, far across the compound, a group of men were hosing down a small building. No one was paying them any attention.

The blades were whirling and the craft hummed and shuddered. Then it lifted off.

Hog yelled in glee, "I think we done it!"

"By George," Loughlin said grandly, "yes, I think we fucking done it."

Harris piloted the craft away from the compound, barely clearing the bamboo wall, then lifting.

Stone gazed back and his grip relaxed on the automatic rifle.

Right—they *had* done it.

Lerida would never be the same. The Sandinistas would never put any gold stars next to their names.

Hog grinned like a crazy man.

"We head for Honduras, right?"

"Wouldn't have it any other way," Stone said.

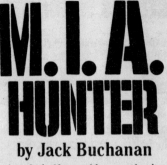

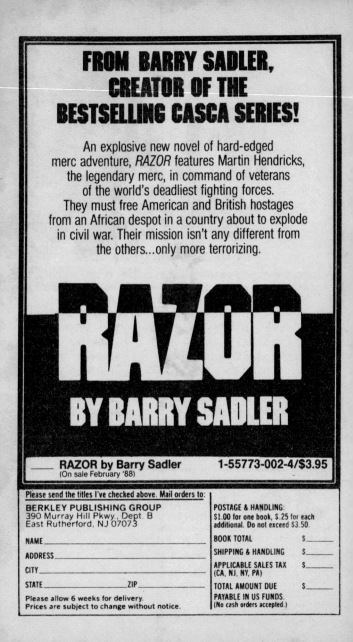